FINDING CHRISTMAS

Dear Wonderful Peeps,

Hope you enjoy the read!

Please help me spread the word. Praying for you always!

Big hugs,

D

FINDING CHRISTMAS

written by

Donna Douglas Walchle

Published by

Donna D Here Publishing

Editor: Dr. Julie Anne Cross

Cover Design: Winnie Clark

Library of Congress Control Number: 2019915657

ISBN 978-0-9891123-4-5

Also by Donna I. Douglas/Donna Douglas Walchle

God Stories: They're So Amazing Only God Could Make Them Happen

Make Lemonade

Winks from God

There's an Owl in the Closet

Please visit:

www.donnadhere.com

To the best Mommie in the world…thank you. And to Jim, my wonderful husband and favorite date EVER! I never knew what I was missing. It was you all along. I love you.

Big hugs,

D

Contents

Preface

At some point or another, everyone stands alone on a clear night gazing upward at an array of countless glistening stars sprayed against a black velvet sky. This vast canopy of unexcelled beauty causes wonder to rise up in our spirit rendering even the most cynical among us awestruck.

It's that feeling of discovery or being in on a private reveal offered by invitation only. It's an encounter that takes your breath away and will forever be indelibly imprinted on your heart and in your memory. This is the result of one unpretentious principal... seeking and finding.

Sam Waters has completely detached from even the remotest interest in seeking and finding. He's forgotten how it feels to wonder or to be captivated by anything or anyone. In fact truth be told, he's lost his way altogether.

For years now he's cut himself off from living. He's become a hermit of sorts. He's given up on love and on life. But, Love and Life have never given up on him and in fact on a daily basis both continue to chase after him. Because of that relentless pursuit his controlled, elected isolation status is about to all change. And that change will come through one simple means...finding Christmas.

Finding Christmas

Music and Lyrics by Donna I. Douglas and Cheryl Rogers

It's more than a time

For getting together

With family and friends

More than stockings by the fire

Twinkling lights and decorations

More than Santa Claus

Or candles and wreaths

So much more than all the presents

Underneath the tree

Finding Christmas

Changes everything

No more searching

No more wandering

It's comfort and joy

It's hope and peace

And love just waiting to be found

By opening this perfect gift

And finding Christmas

A star in the East

Lit up the heavens

For this newborn king

A manger in a stable

Became a throne where angels sang

Shepherds and wisemen

Bowed down before the Christ

The Savior God had promised

Was right before their eyes

Finding Christmas

Changes everything

No more searching

No more wandering

It's comfort and joy

It's hope and peace

And love just waiting to be found

By opening this perfect gift

And finding Christmas

Chapter 1

It is a crisp, cool, day break in Atlanta, Georgia as the peach and yellow hues of sunrise peak over the horizon. A sea of headlights from various interstates flow like sludge as early morning workers make their way into the city. The rooftops of several skyscrapers host brightly decorated, well-lit, fifty-foot Christmas trees and glowing, jovial snowmen and snowwomen who seem to cast a friendly wave to all the passersby. Decorative wreaths, garland and lights are plentiful and draped across office buildings reflecting the festivities of the holiday season.

Peeling off into the city streets are cars, buses and taxis still in the hustle-bustle of faithful commuters. They display creative vehicle decorations, a host of seasonal reminders that Christmas cheer is in the air. Joggers in their holiday sweat suits, cozy sweaters, scarves and caps, dart in and out of chilly pedestrians briskly making their way to work via the wide, city sidewalks.

But, not everyone is preparing to celebrate Christmas. In fact, Sam Waters—youthful mid-fifties, unshaven, dressed in several layers of flannel, sweat pants, worn running shoes, a knit cap and a tattered Army jacket—hasn't celebrated Christmas for a seven years. He has suffered a loss that he just can't seem to get past: the passing of Becca, his beloved wife of thirty years. This morning is no different from all the other mornings since she died. He sits alone in front of a headstone at Northside Cemetery.

Becca Ann Waters

August 8th, 1968–December 20th, 2014

Wife, Mom, Grammy and Friend

"She Loved Well"

He doesn't seem to notice he's surrounded by rows of headstones that cover acres of rolling hills. Many headstones are decorated with Christmas poinsettias and some with garland and Christmas lights. A groundskeeper rakes the last of winter leaves. All alone, Sam quietly cries, occasionally warming his hands by blowing hot air into his cupped fists.

"I miss you, Bec. I miss you every day. But, at Christmas it's worse because you loved everything about Christmas—the decorations, the gifts, the big dinners, singing Christmas carols and that church play they do every year that you always made me sit through—all of it made you so happy."

He cries harder.

"But, I hate Christmas because everything about it reminds me that you're not here. I keep thinking things will get better but they don't. Whoever said that time heals all wounds is a liar!"

Sam wipes his nose with the arm of his jacket and brushes tears from his eyes.

"I'm empty. Nothing moves me anymore, Bec. I can cry but I haven't laughed or felt any happiness in—I can't even remember. I just wish I knew what to do. I need help."

Behind Sam and within earshot stands a mature, distinguished man with a kind face wearing warm winter clothing and a cap with the initials SSV on it. He responds to Sam's private conversation.

"Finally!"

The stranger smiles and winks at him. Startled, Sam turns to inspect the intruder.

"Who are you? And where'd you come from?"

Sam surveys the surroundings, making sure the man doesn't have accomplices. The kind stranger sits down beside him and extends his hand to shake it. Sam hesitantly complies.

"I'm SSV."

"SSV?"

"That's right. SSV. Your Still Small Voice. You know! The one that nudges you when you need to be coaxed to move ahead and puts the brakes on when you need to be cautioned or protected?"

Sam looks skeptical, completely taken aback and alternates mumbling to himself and responding to SSV.

"My Still Small Voice? Yeah, right. Great! You know what I always say, nothing like starting out the day with a delusional crazy person! But, I'll play along. Where'd you come from, Still Small Voice?"

SSV smiles knowingly.

"I'm always here."

"Well, one of us is high as a kite. And, it's not me."

Completely incensed, Sam quickly jumps to his feet and raises his fists, posing like a prizefighter. SSV stands and calmly faces his opposition.

"Now you look, whoever you are, I don't know if you just escaped from a psych ward, or what kind of scam you're running, but you need to leave—now!!"

The groundskeeper gazes over at the commotion, which appears to be Sam air fighting and talking to himself. He resumes raking. Sam relaxes his stance as SSV calmly replies.

"Sorry, Sam. But, I can never leave you."

"How do you know my name?"

"I know everything about you, Sam."

"Yeah, like what?"

"You came from meager beginnings, but started and built the largest privately held real estate company in the country. You're a workaholic. Your business savvy is unsurpassed, but your people skills, not so much."

"My reputation and accomplishments are public information! Not impressed."

"Your wife was your best friend and biggest cheerleader. In fact, she was a cheerleader to many and was masterful at developing relationships. She loved people and helping those in need. It's how she spent her life—by investing her heart and resources into people."

Sam boldly points to himself.

"Well, it takes money to fill needs you know. How do you think that happens? I'll tell you how— this workaholic made that happen!"

"Your son is a trust fund baby who has never held a job in his life, mostly due to your lack of parenting."

"Lack of parenting? He had a private education, a brand new car when he turned sixteen, college completely paid for—he had everything."

"Everything but your guidance, discipline and approval. Everything, but you."

"Becca always coddled him. She's the one who made him weak."

"She overcompensated because you were never there. And, blaming Becca when she's not even here to defend herself? Sam, really? That issue's always been a challenge for you, too."

"What issue?"

"Not accepting responsibility for your blunders."

Sam goes mute and awaits the continuance of truth telling. SSV is just getting started.

"You're estranged from your daughter, Callie because she married a minister whose income potential was beneath your expectations. "

"She deserved better!"

"She was in love with Jack."

Staring mindlessly into space and privately recounting days gone by, Sam shakes his head in clueless disbelief and responds emphatically, "Love is so over-rated."

"First, you hired a private detective to catch Jack in the act of...only your imagination knows what. Then, after learning all he was guilty of was visiting people in hospitals, feeding the homeless and leading a youth group at church, you came up empty."

"Do you know what pastors make? How could she just settle like that?"

"You're private investigation failed, so next, you offered to buy Jack off with an obscene amount of money—if he'd leave town never to be seen again. But, he refused."

Still not understanding the measure of his contemptible attempts at persuasion, Sam voices an outcome he deems honorable to layer his debate and responds, "He could have started a nice little business with that money. Made something of himself."

SSV shakes his head at Sam's inability to see beyond his myopic viewpoint.

"Finally, in one last-ditch effort, you offered Callie her trust fund early and threw in an entire summer touring Europe if she'd only break up with Jack. She turned you down, too."

Clueless to the depth of his manipulation, Sam shakes his head and responds.

"Kids! Shocking, isn't it? Never expected that kind of response. The ignorance of youth, I guess."

"It was something you never expected because up until that moment you've always been able to manipulate people into doing whatever you want by simply writing a check. But, much to your dismay, some people, including Callie and Jack, can't be bought. Love won out. Love always wins, Sam."

"In all fairness to me, Becca had just died and I was really in a bad place."

"So was Callie, Sam. And you deserted her."

"No, she deserted me. Callie and Jack eloped, you know!"

"Do you blame them?"

Becoming pensive, Sam answers quietly.

"Then, they moved away—far away. Probably intentional."

"Jack accepted a position at a church in Texas. Shall I continue?"

"What's left?"

"Oh, there's a whole lifetime of details to reel off. How about your grandchildren? Can you tell me their names or birthdays?"

"My personal assistant keeps up with all that."

"Exactly."

"Well, you could have found out all of this information from just about anyone. So, who was your source?"

"I'm the source, Sam. I know what I know because I know—everything."

Sam kisses the fingertips of his right hand, touches the top of the headstone and looks sternly at SSV as they walk together.

"In other words, you're a know-it-all! This all sounds very suspicious—crazy, really. You appear out of nowhere and tell me you're all-knowing and my still small voice..."

"Yes. And so, I'm making myself a little less still and a little less small to help you. You've lost your way, Sam."

"Well, I don't need your help!"

Item by item, SSV matter-of-factly rattles off the list, using his fingers to count.

"That's not what you just said to Becca. You said and I'm quoting, 'I'm empty. Nothing moves me anymore. I can cry but I haven't laughed or felt any happiness in—I can't even remember. I just wish I knew what to do. I need help.'"

"Look, I was just having an intimate conversation with my wife."

"Your wife who passed away years ago? Sam, you've always worked hard and been a great provider for your family. Flawed as you are, you've been well-intentioned. But, since Becca died, you've been completely shut down. Life and living is all around you. And you're missing it."

"I hadn't noticed."

"Exactly. That's the point, Sam."

Sam stops in his tracks, turns and faces SSV.

"Look, I don't know what kind of game you're playing or who hired you to follow me, but you need to go back where you came from. This entire conversation has been disturbing, to say the least!"

"Sam, I'm where I've always been. It's just that until today, you've never asked for help. My job is not to force you into anything or to insist on my own ways. My job is to guide and direct you. Whether you listen or implement my suggestions is always your choice."

"Do you know how ridiculous you sound?"

Smiling and very patient, SSV answers. "Not the first time I've been rejected. But, Sam if you're opened to listening to me, I really can help you make your life better and make you better at life."

"And how do you plan on doing that?"

SSV gently places his hand on Sam's shoulder. Sam gazes at his hand and then looks at him eye to eye.

"You want a preview, huh? I like that. Ok, before going home today, take a stroll through town. Open your eyes, ears and heart to the needs of the people you encounter. View life as it exists outside of yourself. See how it resonates."

"That sounds like a ludicrous waste of time!"

"Always your choice, Sam."

Sam furrows his brow and contemplates the comment. When he looks back at SSV, he's gone. Sam does a 360° turn, looking in all directions. Perplexed, he continues walking on a path by rows of headstones and then out of the front gates.

Chapter 2

Against his better judgment and more an issue of curiosity than anything, Sam decides to make his way into town and to observe only God knows what. The city traffic is still bumper-to-bumper and the shrill cacophony of car horns sound like an orchestra tuning up. Street light poles are wrapped in silver garland with red and green bells. The exterior of most high-rise offices and sky scrappers are decorated for Christmas.

Tall, beautifully trimmed Christmas trees are visible through scenic window-fronts. Wide city sidewalks are populated with people in winter wear, scurrying to work. Sam blends into the crowd as he continues walking. He observes a department store with eager employees outside hanging a banner that says, "MERRY CHRISTMAS." Sam passes by.

A tall church steeple he hasn't noticed in years reflects the morning sun. Beneath it on ground level is a life-size manger scene. The church marquee says, "COME CELEBRATE JESUS."

Sam gazes across the street at Midtown hospital. He spent many weeks there when Becca was sick. Momentarily, he reflects on her illness, her suffering and the unfairness of it all. Quickly, he puts all of those unpleasant memories out of his mind: the ones that still keep him up at night. They must be stored away and deeply buried in a compartment that can't reach him. He knows all too well the damage those images cause and for a brief moment thinks about the people on the inside who are going through similar circumstances.

One of those people is Janee Williams, a school bus driver, African American, jovial, fiftyish who stands beside the bed of her husband, Rich, a cancer patient. Rich, late fifties and gaunt from the effects of this evil predator, is asleep wearing an oxygen mask and hooked up to a plethora of IV's. Janee holds his hand and kisses his forehead.

"I'll be back after work. I love you."

She leaves Rich's room, exits out the front entrance of the hospital and down the steps toward the parking lot. There, Janee approaches a big, yellow school bus, opens the door, climbs in and sits in the driver's seat. She fires it up and slowly pulls away.

Sam stands in a line of a half dozen people, buys a cup of coffee and then continues walking toward a fire barrel. Several people encircle the barrel and warm their hands. Sam stops to warm his, momentarily observes the people around him, looks perplexed and walks on. Unbeknownst to him, SSV trails behind, stops to warm his hands and then continues following Sam.

In a nearby suburb is the Martinez house. It's in ill repair, paint chipping, gutters full and falling. The lawn is full of leaves from the bare oak tree. The walkway is cracked and covered with the residue of faded chalk art. A ten-year-old SUV in need of new tires is backed in the driveway and facing the street.

Inside, the kitchen has dated appliances, Formica counter tops, old light fixtures and antiquated wallpaper. Diann Martinez—attractive, mid-thirties, dressed for work—and her three children: Matthew, twelve, Harper, eight and Jesse, ten, are all dressed for school. They huddle before an IPAD to talk with their husband and father, Army Captain Harry Martinez, who is handsome, late thirties, and serving in the Middle East.

"We love you, honey. You're all we want for Christmas!"

"I'll be there! I love all of you, too. You kids take care of Mama. Gotta go now."

"Ok! We will Daddy! We love you!"

Residing next door to the Martinez's, is a petite, silver haired, feisty eighty-year-old widow that everyone affectionately calls Aunt Ginny. But for a porch and yard full of leaves, her house is in impeccable condition.

Aunt Ginny sits in her kitchen drinking hot tea and eating a piece of toast and some fruit. Next to her is a place setting with a coffee cup, plate and silverware. She butters a piece of toast and puts it on the plate next to her. She talks to the empty chair as though she was having breakfast with a friend.

Suddenly, she hears the commotion of her next-door neighbors leaving and makes her way to her large living room window. Aunt Ginny peeks through the blinds, watching Diann and the Martinez children, carrying book bags and packed lunches, as they make their way out of the house to the SUV. She crosses her fingers and raises her hands toward heaven like she's rooting for the home team.

"C'mon, Bertha. C'mon, now. C'mon."

All of the car doors close in sync. Everyone bows their heads as Diann prays.

"Lord, please help old Bertha to start this morning. You know she doesn't do too well in the cold. Amen."

All three kids cross their fingers as Diann attempts to start the old dinosaur. After several unsuccessful attempts, Bertha finally starts. The kids begin shouting and clapping; next-door, Aunt Ginny continues boosting both arms in the air and rejoices right along with them!

"Yes! Thank you, Lord! You got that old rattletrap started one more time! Now, please keep 'em safe and allow them to reach their destination one more time!"

The SUV pulls down the driveway and quickly drives off.

Still trying to make any sense of SSV's suggestion to roam through town and observe the people, Sam approaches a massive high-rise that covers half a city block. He sits drinking his coffee on the lower steps of the broad, expansive stone steps leading up to the impressive entrance. A Salvation Army bell ringer stationed at the top of the stairs just outside the entrance rings her bell.

Pastor Jack Thornsby of Midtown Church, a handsome man in his early thirties, pushes his five- year-old daughter, Megan in a manually operated, rickety wheelchair. She seems quite precocious and uninhibited by her disability. They are headed in Sam's direction, toward the bus stop on the corner.

Megan spots Sam, gives him a long gaze and assesses that he is homeless. She tugs on her dad's coat sleeve and turns to say something to him as she searches through her lunch box.

"Daddy, that man looks hungry. I want to share my sandwich."

They pull up to where Sam sits. Megan hands Sam half a sandwich and fearlessly addresses Sam.

"I'm sharing half my sandwich with you, Mister. My mama made it and she's a really good sandwich maker."

Hesitantly and to be gracious, Sam takes the sandwich and has a bite.

"Thank you," Sam says humbly.

Pastor Jack recognizes Sam but Sam does not recognize him. Pastor Jack and Megan continue on toward the bus stop. Pastor Jack bends down to compliment Megan.

"I'm proud of you for wanting to help that man. You have a good heart, Megan."

Megan smiles broadly.

Sam watches the two walking away as SSV sits down next to him on the opposite side.

"Didn't recognize them, did you?"

Startled, Sam jumps and spills a bit of his coffee.

"You gotta stop dropping in like this!"

"Can't stop, Sam. It's what I do."

"And no, I didn't recognize them. But, I'm sure you're going to enlighten me."

"The man pushing the wheel chair is Pastor Jack Thornsby. Ring a bell?"

Sam stares at SSV, then looks back at Jack and Megan.

"The last time I saw Callie, she told me that she loves me but that I owed her and particularly her husband an apology. And until that happens she would maintain her boundaries."

"And, you've remained mute all this time."

"Yes."

"Why do you think you never tried to make amends?"

"What happened to 'judge not?'"

"Not judging, just asking."

"I really don't think they want to have anything to do with me."

"Well, they've moved back to town so whether or not they want anything to do with you doesn't have to remain a mystery. The ball's in your court, Sam, just like it's always been. Jack's the pastor at Midtown Church. And Megan, the little girl in the wheel chair is your granddaughter."

Taken aback, Sam strains to get another glimpse.

"My granddaughter? Callie's a mother? You're kidding! Why didn't anyone let me know?"

A half-dozen children accompanied by parents wait as the bus approaches and stops. Janee releases her stop guards and opens the door. The children begin boarding as Janee cheerfully greets them.

"Good morning, children!"

"Good morning," they reply back in unison.

Janee lowers the lift, Pastor Jack rolls Megan onto it and she is raised onto the bus as Janee talks with Pastor Jack through the open door.

"How're you two doing this morning?

We're doing fine, Janee. How's Rich doing?

"Doctors say he's holding his own."

Pastor Jack smiles empathetically and nods.

"Good to hear. I'll check in on him."

"Thank you, Pastor Jack. I know he'd like to see you."

Sam continues observing from a distance as the bus door closes. Pastor Jack and the other parents wave as the bus pulls away in the direction of Sam. Pastor Jack looks around for a safe hiding place in hopes to further observe Sam a little more.

As the bus passes Sam and SSV, Megan peers out of the window and waves to Sam. Sam waves back as SSV points out the obvious.

"You know, it's nothing short of a miracle when something you've lost is found, Sam."

Sam continues to follow the bus with his eyes and solemnly asks a question.

"Why is Megan in a wheel chair?"

"She loves horses, just like the rest of the Waters clan. She's ridden since almost before she could walk. She was learning to jump. The horse stumbled."

Momentarily overcome, Sam becomes emotional.

From behind the city bus stop petition, Pastor Jack watches Sam who uses overt hand motions, as he responds to SSV (who is still invisible to everyone else).

"Yeah, well what am I supposed to do with that 'intel' as you call it? I haven't seen my daughter in years! I can't just pop in on her; that's your style, not mine."

Pastor Jack is wide-eyed watching Sam talk to himself.

"Eyes, ears and heart open, Sam. They've all got to be open. Very key."

SSV stands and walks away. Sam watches him, stands and points, jabbing with his index finger as he hurls one more comment.

"Oh, yeah, well you could be a little more detailed with your instructions, you know! Can you do that? Think of yourself as the Still Small Voice of GPS! Specifics! I need specifics!"

Pastor Jack shakes his head and mumbles to himself, "This can't be good."

Sam walks to the end of the block then between two high rise buildings and down an alley void of people. The red tail lights of a white late model Bentley illuminate as it begins backing out of an alley onto the side street where it is parallel to the buildings on both sides.

Cyrus, the chauffeur, sixty, distinguished good looks, wearing a dark suit and tie gets out and opens the rear passenger side door. Sam walks up to the car, gets in and Cyrus closes the door. He walks back around to the driver's seat and gets in.

"Where to sir?"

"Home, Cyrus."

Chapter 3

Awaiting Sam in the backseat cup holder is his favorite coffee in a tall thermal mug. Sam closes his eyes, inhales and then reaches for the java. He takes a long slow sip and opens the business journal that Cyrus has strategically placed on the seat for his perusal. Sam realizes that these gestures were intentional.

"My favorite coffee. Thank you, Cyrus. And, for the journal."

Feeling accomplished and responding proudly with eye contact in the rear view mirror, "My pleasure, sir."

Suddenly, SSV appears in the back seat next to Sam. Sam seems almost resigned.

"Nice ride, Sam, and good of you to compliment Cyrus for bringing along your favorite coffee."

"We've got to stop meeting like this!"

Slightly confused, Cyrus responds, "Sir?"

Sam looks sternly at SSV.

"Nothing Cyrus. Just mumbling to myself."

SSV pushes the envelope and decides to challenge Sam a bit.

"Sam, at Christmas, when Becca was alive, your house was decorated like a winter wonderland! Just beautiful! Something as simple as reinstating that tradition would reflect the joy and celebration of Christmas and honor Becca's legacy. It would also make your staff extremely happy. They all used to look forward to being a part of that."

"I hate Christmas decorations!"

"Yes sir, we all know that. And we all respect your prerogative," Cyrus says.

Sam rolls his eyes in frustration and nods to acknowledge Cyrus's response before rolling up the window between them. He then takes out his cell phone and puts it up to his ear.

"Why are you pretending to make a call?" SSV inquires.

"I'm pretending to make a call so when I talk to you it doesn't appear that I've lost my mind sitting back here talking to myself!"

SSV laughs and then continues his cheerleading session.

"Look, Sam, a lot of people miss Becca. She had such a big heart, and was such a lover of people and a generous giver. You have the opportunity to pick up where she left off."

"If it were up to me, I'd just skip Christmas. It's depressing."

"Sam, you have much more to accomplish in life. You've been blessed with the resources to change peoples lives. But in order to do that you've got to be willing to make some changes yourself."

"Changes? Like what?"

SSV holds out his left palm and uses his right index finger to emulate writing.

"Here's your first clue. Note to self: it's not always about you."

Sam, completely incensed, turns to respond. But SSV is gone.

The Bentley approaches the gates surrounding the Waters Estate. Sam's home is a beautiful, stone and brick, 15,000 ft. palatial mansion set back from the road on ten acres of pristinely manicured grounds. An ornately designed wrought iron railing surrounds a large fountain, central to the circular driveway in front of the house.

There's a large pool area behind the house. The pool is covered for the winter as is the outside kitchen adjacent to the cabana house. Tennis courts are set behind the pool area and accessed by a pebble pathway. Detached from the house, the eight-car garage doors are opened revealing Sam's impressive car collection.

Horse stables surrounded by white fences rest on a couple acres to the side of the property. Large riding corrals with jumping mounts sit to the side of the stable. On the opposite side, several beautiful horses graze inside the fences.

Inside the modern, industrial-sized kitchen, Marianna conducts a staff meeting. She is in her late forties, beautiful and impeccably dressed: she was Becca's best friend since childhood and is Sam's personal assistant. The staff, includes the housekeeper, Belle, who is mid-fifties, plump, jolly and married to the chauffeur, Cyrus. The personal chef, Francie—forty, petite and full of energy—and the grounds keeper, Manny—mid-thirties, quiet and dedicated—complete the group. All but Cyrus are in attendance. Marianna stands before them.

"When Mr. Waters returns from his graveside visit he will sign all of the donation checks to charities and Christmas bonuses for company employees and household staff. As all of you know, when Mrs. Waters was alive it was a very joyful occasion and her favorite day of the year. She loved giving and relished delivering the checks to all of the charities. And, then afterwards, she'd come home and decorate for Christmas—to the max—inside and out. I've never seen a more beautiful house!"

Fondly, everyone smiles and nods.

Francie reminisces, "And we all loved listening to the laughter coming from the family room when the two of you decorated the tree! It sounded like two little girls."

Composed, but unable to keep the tears from emerging, Marianna contemplates the statement.

"Well, she was my first friend in a new town at a new school when we were eight. She was my oldest and best friend. I miss her every day."

She collects herself and gets back to business.

"But, Christmas is not the same for Mr. Waters. It's a sad time for him because he misses his wife and wants anything that would remind him of her and her love of Christmas to be kept at bay. Let's do our best to remember that and to make it a special day for him."

"I'm making his favorite breakfast!" Francie gleefully responds.

"Fresh sheets are on his bed! I put the plush white spa towels in his ensuite and his bathroom floor is heated for him. And, Cyrus brought along a thermos of his favorite coffee and a business journal for his ride this morning," says Belle.

"Wonderful!" exclaims Marianne.

Manny chimes in, "The grounds are in tip- top shape, just like he likes them. Horses are all brushed and fed."

"I just wish we could decorate like we did when Mrs. Waters was alive. Everything was so gorgeous," says Belle.

"Well, maybe someday—but until he decides, let's just continue being understanding."

"Well, at least he still allows me to prepare a traditional Christmas dinner with all the trimmings," Francie shares with relief.

Everyone laughs. Marianna looks at her iPad for scheduling.

"Speaking of Christmas dinner, Mr. Waters' son, Robert, his wife and two children will be visiting in route to Aspen. Francie, check with Mr. Waters to set the menu. Thank you so much for all of your good work and kindness!"

The Bentley makes its way down the long driveway and parks in the circular drive in front of the house. Sam and Cyrus exit the car and go inside.

The ebony, Macassar dining room floor is covered with a custom-made tapestry rug. Atop the rug is a twenty-foot burled walnut dining table with sixteen ribbon back chairs. A massive rosewood china cabinet on one wall is filled with royal crown derby china and serving pieces. Two ornately decorated antique curio cabinets filled with collectables are on either side of a stunning mahogany side table. A sterling silver coffee service is centered on the side table flanked by two sterling silver candelabras.

Sam enters the dining room and sits at the head of the table before an elegant, handmade lace placemat, linen napkins and silverware. A china coffee cup sits beside a sterling coffee pot. Sam helps himself to a cup of coffee and continues perusing his business journal as he awaits breakfast.

Francie enters carrying a china plate with a sterling silver plate cover. She pulls off the cover and serves Sam an egg white vegetable omelet, a cup of oatmeal with blueberries and a piece of rye toast. She refreshes his coffee.

"Your favorite, Sir."

"It looks great, Francie. Could you ask Marianna to join me?"

"Certainly."

Francie, exits and in short order, Marianna enters. Sam stands to pull out her chair.

"Good morning, Sam!"

"Good morning, Marianna."

"Is everything ok?"

His look is solemn, almost reverent. Marianna sits quietly, trying to read the unusual timidity from this usually predictable and emphatically strong-willed man in charge.

"Not really. Are you aware that Callie's moved back to town?"

"I am."

"Well, why didn't you say anything?

"It's her news, not mine. I'm not getting in the middle."

"Well, how long has she been back?"

"That's another question you'll have to ask her. How did you find out?"

"This dude I met—it's kind of hard to explain, but he pointed out to me my son-in-law and granddaughter. I didn't even know she existed. Did you?"

"Yes. I know about Megan. My relationship with Callie has never changed, Sam. I talk to her several times a week and have flown out to see her, Jack and Megan many times."

"Well, how could you keep something like that a secret? "

"I was honoring Callie's wishes. "

"She is so stubborn! Just like her mother."

"Really? Her mother? You might want to rethink that!"

SSV laughs.

"What do you mean?"

"Sam, please indulge me. You're missing out on so many wonderful things. Things that you would love and that you should be a part of. And it's because you're stubborn. You're one apology away from a whole lot of wonderful."

"She disrespected me. She went against my wishes."

"She's guilty of falling in love. And just FYI—they're still in love and have a great life together. They're happy. But, there's something missing. It's you. Fix it, Sam. You know it's what Becca would want."

Sam contemplates her comments and changes the subject. His tone is soft and somewhat monotone as though from one who finds himself completely out of his comfort zone.

"Speaking of what Becca would want—I'd like the staff to decorate for Christmas this year."

Stunned and excited, but respectful of the inner debate at she knows went into this decision, Marianna excitedly reacts.

"Outside and inside?"

SSV sits at the head of the opposite end of the table and feels the need to add some "intel."

"Becca and Marianna used to decorate the tree in the family room. Maybe you and Marianna could work on that?"

Drawing a line in the sand Sam quickly says, "Don't push it!"

Thinking Sam is speaking to her, Marianna humbly backs off.

"Oh, Sam, please forgive me. I didn't mean to overstep."

Thrown by SSV's comment, Sam recovers quickly and conveys his desires.

"No, please, you didn't overstep anything— not at all. Both—by all means both—inside and outside. Just like Becca would have done it.

And, how about you and I work on decorating the Christmas tree in the family room?"

"Wonderful! I'd like that!"

Sam finishes his breakfast and stands to exit. Marianna stands as well and is reservedly excited at the hint that Sam's apathetic spirit is becoming slightly infused with a subtle amount of restored joy.

"Let me get cleaned up. Are the checks ready to sign?"

"On your desk in the study. And when you finish signing the ones for the charities, I'm happy to deliver them."

SSV chimes in.

"That's something you should consider doing, Sam. Meet the people—see the good your contributions are making. Get beyond the superficial!"

Sam stares at SSV as Marianna looks to Sam for a response. She turns to see why he is fixed on the opposite end of the table and then looks back at him.

"This year, I think I will deliver those myself. You pass out the checks here at the house and oversee the decorations. Arrange for a courier to pick up the ones for the office. When I get back we'll trim the tree together."

"One of the checks is for Midtown Church. Maybe you'll see Callie. Maybe today is the day?"

Without expression, Sam hoists his coffee cup. SSV stands close by smiling and pleased with the movement in attitude. Holding her iPad to her chest, Marianna watches Sam exit, looks upward smiling and gives a thumbs-up.

Chapter 4

For over one hundred years, the Midtown Church has been a historical beacon of light to many. Their commitment for community involvement with the outreach of love and meeting the needs of the people serves as a welcoming and highly admired connection for other churches to emulate.

A few cars pepper the parking lot including Diann Martinez's run down SUV, Janee's school bus and a vintage Rolls Royce with a foghorn attached to the outside. That classic belongs to Aunt Ginny.

A small but faithful group is gathered in the fellowship hall, preparing a Christmas blessing for a number of underprivileged children. Pictures of Jesus in various settings line the walls. A large decorated Christmas tree occupies one corner. The volunteers finish up wrapping toys and stacking packages by the tree for the annual Christmas toy drive, including Diann (who is both the music and children's minister), Janee and Aunt Ginny. Diann makes an announcement.

"Thank you all so much for helping out with the toy drive. We've adopted several foster care families this year, as well as all of the children at Bethel Children's Home. These gifts are going to bless a lot of children who otherwise would have nothing. So, thank you all for helping."

Janee weighs in.

"And since many of you have always been faithful to sing or play a part in our Christmas play, remember rehearsal is Saturday at 2 pm! Be there or you'll be missin' out! Diann needs all the help she can get!"

In true Aunt Ginny style, she goes directly for the bottom line.

"Janee, I can't sing or act so I can't help you! Wrapping gifts is the extent of my talent!"

Callie, Pastor Jack's wife—and Sam's estranged daughter, late twenties, cute with a bubbly personality, dressed in sweats—enters pushing a cart on wheels with more wrapped gifts. She adds her two cents.

"Well then, Aunt Ginny, just make a joyful noise, right, choir director?"

Diann smiles and nods affirmatively.

"Absolutely, Callie. A joyful noise goes a long way, Aunt Ginny!"

"Well, my joyful noise would probably cause people to evacuate the building! Let's spare them, shall we?"

Everyone laughs, completes their gift wrapping and begin to disperse as Pastor Jack enters and approaches Callie. He pulls her a few feet away to share the earlier events of the day.

"You're not going to believe who I saw today?"

"Who?"

"Your dad."

"My dad? Where?"

"Sitting on the steps to the entrance of an office building. He was unshaven and wearing old clothes. He didn't look good, Callie. Megan thought he was homeless. She gave him half of her sandwich."

"Did he take it?"

"He did. He even took a bite of the sandwich right in front of us. And, after I put Megan on the bus I stood behind a city bus stop where he couldn't see me and watched him for a minute. It looked like he was talking to himself–agitated, using hand motions and everything."

"I'm sure Marianna would have called us."

"Well, what if he had a stroke or something, who knows? And I know he never liked me but wouldn't you think he would have recognized me?"

Callie stares pensively.

Outside in the church parking lot Diann has the hood of her SUV raised with steam pouring out. Janee exits the building, approaches and stands with Diann as she talks on the phone with AAA.

"Yes, my AAA membership number is 98427813. I'm the wife of an Army Captain serving in the Middle East. Yes, thank you. We are hoping he'll be home for Christmas! It would be the best gift the kids and I could ask for. Yes, same place, same car; the Midtown Church parking lot. Thank you."

As Diann ends the conversation, Janee hugs her.

"It's pretty bad when I call AAA for help so much that they recognize my voice!"

"Well it beats a car note! I say, drive 'em till they drop!"

"We're trying to save and pay cash for a new used one. Definitely don't want to make payments!"

"I hear that!"

"How's that sweet hubby of yours?"

"His doctors say he's holding his own. We're still not sure if he's coming home for Christmas. But we're trusting God! What do you hear from Harry?"

"He's supposed to be home in time for Christmas. That's all the kids and I want."

"We all want that, sweetie!"

Aunt Ginny approaches.

"You need a ride anywhere?"

"Thank you, no. I'm waiting on AAA. Aunt Ginny, I thought you had your license suspended for speeding?"

Aunt Ginny winks and smiles as she gets into her Rolls Royce.

"Oh, you can't believe everything you hear, dear."

Aunt Ginny backs out of the parking space and toots her foghorn. It blares loudly and alerts the masses from several city blocks away. She smiles mischievously and waves as she pulls away. Janee and Diann laugh.

"I bet having her as your next door neighbor is a trip!"

"Actually, she's a complete delight. But, she peeks through her blinds and talks to the kids without opening her door. Says she likes to make them think she's a little crazy. She thinks it keeps them on their toes, helps them behave and gives them the tools to deal with some of the challenges in life."

They laugh.

"Well, since I know AAA is on the way and you are certain to be rescued, I'm going to head on to the hospital to check on my man."

They hug. Janee makes her way to her school bus and drives away.

Chapter 5

The Waters estate is beginning to look a lot like Christmas. Manny is assisted by several other workers, who are up on ladders hanging Christmas lights. Belle hangs an evergreen wreath on the front door as Cyrus and Sam pass her en route to the car. Sam carries a few envelopes and Cyrus opens the rear door for Sam to enter.

As the car door closes, Sam observes the decorations going up, smiles slightly and then is saddened. He looks straight ahead and fights becoming too emotional. They pull away to do something Sam has never been a part of: rather than merely just signing the donation checks, he's on his maiden voyage to deliver them.

Their first stop will be at the Solomon School. The Bentley pulls up and parks at the side of the school. Sam exits the car carrying an envelope. He walks past a fenced playground filled with elementary-aged children. Harper sits alone on a bench close to the fence. She' s crying. A teacher notices and sits beside her. SSV stands on the outside of the fence within earshot and motions Sam to join him.

"I am so sorry, sir. I'm not paying attention to what I'm doing."

Looking around and reading signs, SSV stands next to Sam.

"I don't know what I'm doing either. Do you work here?"

"No, but I'm in here enough to be on their payroll. Where are you trying to go?"

SSV attempts to coach Sam with his lack of social skills.

"Ask her why, Sam. Ask her why she's here enough to be on payroll. The way you get to know people is to ask them questions."

"Why are you here so much?"

"My husband just had his seventh cancer surgery. They're holding him hostage until I pay his tab so I come every day to visit him."

Sam looks horrified. Janee breaks the tension.

"I'm just kidding—about the hostage part, that is. Now, how can I help you?"

Sam is impressed by her positive attitude.

"I need to see the administrator."

"You need to hear this, Sam."

The teacher gently puts her arm around Harper and attempts to get to the source of the tears.

"What's wrong, Harper?"

"Some kids were making fun of me. They say I don't have a Dad."

"Well, you know that's not true. You have a very brave Dad! Did you tell them that?"

"I tried to but they said I was making him up cause they've never seen him."

"Well, we will tell them together. Your dad is a brave soldier who is fighting to protect us and keep us safe. You should be very proud of him. Are you?"

Harper nods and wipes away the tears. The teacher takes Harper by the hand, calls the others playing and they line up to go back inside. Sam is moved but tries to quickly recover. Slightly miffed that SSV thought it necessary to expose him to an innocent little girl who's proud of her daddy and misses him, he gives SSV a long look of displeasure, then walks toward the school entrance to deliver the check.

The Midtown Hospital will be the next stop. Rich lies in a slightly inclined bed hooked up to a overabundance of tubes.

Janee enters, gives him a kiss and stands beside him with her hand on his.

"Hi, Handsome."

Rich is very weak and speaks in a strained whisper.

"Hi, Honey."

"I talked to the doctor. He says you might get to come home for Christmas. We'll just have to wait and see."

"What a Christmas gift—over a $700,000 in medical bills."

"Well, lucky for you, your wife is making the big bucks driving a school bus!"

He smiles. Janee kisses his forehead and squeezes his hand. He drops back off to sleep.

The Bentley pulls up to the hospital and Sam exits carrying an envelope. He enters the hospital and stands by an elevator looking around for clues that might direct him to his desired destination.

The elevator door opens revealing Janee texting on her phone. As she steps off the elevator she rams into Sam who looks lost. Her phone falls to the ground. He retrieves it and hands it back to her.

"That's easy! I've met with her a number of times. Just go straight down this hallway. It's the first door on the left."

"Thank you. Sam. My name is Sam. Sam Waters."

"Janee Williams. Nice to meet you, Sam."

"And your husbands name?"

"Rich. Wait a minute. I remember you! You're Becca Waters husband."

"That's right. You knew Becca?"

"Very well. She went to our church. And when she was here in the hospital I visited her every time I came to see Rich. I believe when she was here, Rich was in for his third bout with cancer."

"And now this is his seventh cancer surgery?"

"That's right."

"Well, I hope he gets better."

Janee lunges forward and hugs Sam.

"I'm so sorry for your loss," Sam.

Janee, slightly embarrassed by her own impulsiveness tries to offer an apology. "And sorry for the hug, if you're not a hugger. It's a knee-jerk reaction."

"No worries. Thank you for the directions. And all the best to you and Rich."

Janee smiles and makes her way toward the exit. Sam heads down the hall toward the administration office. SSV puts his arm around Sam's shoulder. Sam looks at SSV's hand, then at SSV and resigned, continues walking.

The next drop-off destination is Bethel Children's Home. The Bentley pulls up in the front of the home. Sam exits holding an envelope and enters the building. He's inside about twenty minutes before returning to the car and heading to the next stop.

The Food Bank was an organization that Becca contributed to all year long. The Bentley pulls up to the entrance. Sam exits the car holding an envelope and enters the building. When he returns, it is noticeable that his countenance is beginning to change. Perhaps he's beginning to understand why Becca loved giving and serving others.

As Cyrus opens the car door for Sam, Sam becomes emotional when Cyrus informs him of their next destination—the Children's Cancer Research Center. SSV puts his arm around Sam to offer comfort. Cancer seems to be the evil invader that is in some way affecting every person on the planet either directly or indirectly.

But, the children—the children affected—is something Sam will never understand. He remembers how every year Becca chaired the big fundraiser, that is until her own cancer stopped her in her tracks. He has to put that thought away. He has a check to drop off. Once inside, this stop lasts a little longer than the others.

Finally, the Bentley pulls up to the last stop. It's the Midtown Church. This is where Callie's husband is the pastor. What if he's in there? What if she is? Will he meet his young granddaughter today? Hesitant and very nervous, Sam gets out holding an envelope. He stands by the car looking at the church. He slowly walks toward the entrance, stops, then does an about face and gets back in the car. The car drives away.

Inside the Bentley, Sam holds the last envelop and stares straight ahead. He jumps as SSV appears in the seat next to him.

"So close," says SSV.

Sam closes the window between the back and front seat and takes out his phone. SSV playfully does the same.

"It just didn't feel like the right time."

SSV smiles compassionately and puts his arm around Sam.

"How did you like delivering the checks and meeting the recipients?"

"It was bittersweet."

"Reminded you of Becca?"

Sam nods affirmatively.

"I think Becca would be very pleased. You honored her and God by demonstrating His love in a practical way—just like she always did."

A nerve is hit and Sam explodes.

"Don't talk to me about God!"

SSV listens patiently. Cyrus occasionally glances in his rear view through the glass petition to observe his obviously upset boss and wonders who he could be talking with that has him so on fire.

"I asked God for one thing—one simple thing. And He ignored me!"

"You asked Him to heal Becca."

"Yes! I did! You'd think that would be a fairly simple request for the One who created the universe! But, no! That didn't happen."

"I guess that depends on your definition of healed."

"She was sick and I wanted her well. That's the definition of healed!"

"Well, she is healed and whole and perfect. Where she is cancer can never touch her again. So you see, Sam, God did answer your prayer."

"But she's not here, don't you get it?"

"But, she's healed, Sam. And what you did today honors her legacy and that legacy also honors God. You did good, Sam."

Simultaneously, they both put away their phones. They stare straight ahead and ride in silence.

Driving her dilapidated SUV, Diann pulls up to the curb of the Solomon School to pick up her kids just as Janee pulls past with her busload of kids. Janee and Diann wave at each other as Jesse, Matthew and Harper enter the SUV. Diann drives away and begins to inquire about what has happened at school.

"How was your day?"

Harper, still recovering from hurt feelings responds with raw honesty.

"They were mean to me."

"Who was mean to you?"

"Some of the kids in my class. They said I was making up that I had a daddy cuz they've never seen him."

Jesse gives some brotherly advice.

"You can't pay attention to those kind of kids. Just ignore them! They're bullies."

Matthew boldly chimes in.

"Yeah, we know the truth. We not only have a dad, he's a hero!"

Diann echoes the sentiment.

"He sure is! Harper, if I need to speak to your teacher, I can."

"No, my teacher stood up for me and told the bad kids that I did too have a dad who is away serving our country."

"Well, good then. Can anyone tell me something you learned today?"

"I learned that I don't like fractions!" exclaims Jesse.

Everyone laughs as Matthew contributes his answer to the conversation.

"Our class got an assignment for each of us to do one act of kindness before Christmas break."

Harper contemplates a term she's not familiar with.

"What's an act of kindness?"

Somewhat boasting that he knows something she doesn't, he responds, "It's what is sounds like, silly. You just pick someone and do something nice for them."

Now that the dots are connected, Harper fires back,

"Clean my room! That would be something nice."

Everyone laughs as Diann probes further.

"Do you have something in mind?"

"I was thinking about raking the leaves in Aunt Ginny's yard," says Matthew.

"What a lovely idea," Diann says.

Not to be left out, Jesse throws in an offer.

"I'll help you. Aunt Ginny can be kind of scary the way she stares out her window at us and talks through her door."

"Aunt Ginny is harmless," Diann says assuredly.

Not completely convinced, Jesse retorts, "At church she seems normal but when she's at home, she acts kind of weird."

"Yeah, one day we were watching her through her back window and she set a place at the table for—ah—for nobody. And she talked to the empty chair while she ate," Matthew explains.

"Maybe she has an imaginary friend," says Harper in her defense.

Offering insight and a life lesson, Diann replies, "Aunt Ginny probably just misses her husband and having someone to eat with."

"Well, we should invite her over to eat with us! We have an empty chair at our table, too," Harper exclaims.

"But, not for long!" says Matthew with great anticipation.

"That's right. But, we can always add an extra chair any time we want to have Aunt Ginny over. I'm sure she will appreciate having her lawn raked, boys. And, Harper, I had in mind an act of kindness myself. You and I can work on that one together."

Harper smiles and gives and thumbs up.

Chapter 6

The Bentley pulls through the wide double security gates and makes its way down the long, winding drive up to a completely decorated house. Wreaths with red bows hang from all of the windows. Lights are strung all around the outside of the house.

A life-size manger scene is in the front yard. A couple of tall live evergreens are decorated with white lights, large red ornaments and a huge star at the top. Sam and Cyrus examine the perimeter and go inside.

Marianna cheerfully greets Sam and Cyrus at the door and hands Sam and cup of eggnog. He seems slightly take aback, until she explains.

"You can't decorate a Christmas tree without the proper tools. Becca always believed that eggnog was one of those tools!"

Sam smiles and takes a sip. SSV smiles as he observes the interaction. Marianna then guides Sam into the family room. The fireplace is blazing. Garland is draped across the mantle and on top of the mantle is Becca's collection of angels.

Wreaths with red bows are in all of the windows. Candles are tastefully lit throughout the spacious, comfortable room, furnished with a couple of high back chairs, a large couch, a recliner and window seats. A large coffee table holds a manger scene and various sized snowmen and snowwomen are displayed on both end tables.

A baby grand piano occupies one corner and a large, beautiful spruce in another corner is erect in its stand. A large star gloriously crowns the top of the tree and lights are generously draped around the circumference. Several large boxes of ornaments and decorations sit close by on the floor. Marianna playfully looks at Sam, holds up an ornament, places a hook in the top of it and hangs it on the tree.

"And that's how it's done!"

Sam puts down his eggnog and gives ornament hanging a whirl. He successfully hangs a hand-painted angel on just the right branch.

"I think I've got it!"

Sam seems to vaguely recognize the labeling on one of the boxes. He begins rummaging around in it, finds a Santa hat and a beard and puts them on.

Not to be outdone, Marianna grabs a Mrs. Santa cap, wire rimmed glasses and wraps silver garland around her neck like a scarf. They laugh and continue hanging ornaments. Sam throws another log on the fire and they continue decorating the tree until every branch has been generously cared for.

With the fire settling down, Sam and Marianna sit in two high back chairs drinking eggnog and admiring their decorating. Marianna gets up, goes to the piano and plays, "The Christmas Song." Sam stands and moves in closer to watch her play. At the conclusion of her song, he shows her how the piano is self-playing. The piano continues playing as Sam extends his hand toward her and bows. SSV gives a thumbs-up.

"May I have this dance?"

Marianna smiles, takes his hand, stands and complies. As they dance, both seem to be caught up in a swirl of memories that include Becca as well as new thoughts about each other that neither has ever considered, at least not until now.

At the conclusion of the dance, they remove their Santa and Mrs. Claus garb and sit back down by the tree.

"How'd it go today?"

Sam looks puzzled.

"Dropping off the checks to the charities?"

"Oh, it went fine. I met a few people. Talked to a few. It was different than what I expected."

"In what way?"

"Well, I actually got an idea of how the money is used. Put a name with a face with a need."

"How'd it go at Midtown Church?"

Sam is embarrassed.

"We stopped by but I decided not to go in."

"Why?"

"So much time has passed. I don't know. It's awkward."

Marianna raises a brow.

"Why don't you drop off the check to them? It's the donation that they need, not me. That's probably the best I can do."

"No, it's not, Sam. It's not the best you can do. Money's never any competition or a replacement for love and a relationship."

"You sound so much like Becca. She never let me get away with anything."

SSV sits on the couch with his arms crossed, brows raised and a smirk on his face that silently conveys, "I think you've met your match."

"Would you want to come with me?"

"I can. But, you know what to do. It's time, Sam."

"I think I'd feel better if you were with me."

"Happy to."

Marianna stands and takes one more long, approving gaze at the tree.

"That was really fun! It felt like old times. Thank you."

"No, thank you! Where are you headed?"

"Home."

"Do you have dinner plans?"

Marianna smiles and so does SSV as he adjusts one of the ornaments. Sam and Marianna adjourn to the dining room.

Sam sits at the head of the dining room table and Marianna to his right. Francie brings in two plates of salmon, brown rice, broccoli and squash. They eat, talk and have a toast of wine. SSV is at the opposite end of the table and coaches Sam.

"Questions, Sam. Show interest by asking questions."

Sam takes a sip of wine.

"I hope this isn't too personal, but why have you never married?"

SSV shakes his head and mumble to himself.

"That was subtle."

Sam continues.

"I mean, you're beautiful, smart, kind, direct—ah that bears repeating—direct, and after decorating a Christmas tree with you, I can add that you're also a lot of fun."

Well, because I love kids so much, everyone always assumed I'd be the one to marry and have a house full of children. But, it just never happened."

"Ever been in love?"

"Not so far. I've dated a few men that I thought had great promise, but we just ended up becoming good friends. In fact, we still are. And, of course, having children now isn't an option. I'm still opened to the idea of marriage, but to this point, no one has ridden up on a white horse and swept me off my feet."

"A white horse, huh? Well, whoever captures your heart will be one fortunate man."

"Thank you, Sam. And, thank you for rekindling some wonderful memories of decorating the tree with Becca and for this lovely dinner. I guess I'd better get going."

Chapter 7

It's early Saturday morning at the Martinez house. The SUV is backed into the driveway, facing the street. Carrying rakes, Jesse and Matthew run out the front door toward Aunt Ginny's house.

The leaves on the front porch are plentiful. The mounds of leaves in the yard are worse. Jesse and Matthew, shoes buried in fallen leaves up to mid-calf, bravely knock on Aunt Ginny's front door. There's no answer so they knock louder. They wait, but still no answer. They move to the windows on the front porch and try to peer in.

From inside, Aunt Ginny sees them and is mischievously giggling as she hides behind the front door. She responds in her best scary voice.

"Whoooooooo is it?"

Aunt Ginny chuckles to herself knowing full well who it is. The boys move back over in front of the door.

"Aunt Ginny, it's Matthew and Jesse from next door. You know, we go to the same church? We were wondering if we could rake your lawn and sweep your porch?"

Trying to act grouchy to teach them how to deal with difficult people, she challenges them.

"Why would you want to do something nice like that? I'm not paying you for a service I didn't request!"

Matthew attempts to convince her.

"We don't want to get paid. We just want to do something nice for you."

The front door cracks ever so slightly revealing only half of her face.

"Why would you want to do that?"

"It's an act of kindness," Jesse explains.

The door opens a little more.

"No strings attached?"

"No strings."

After a pregnant pause she stuns them as she flings open the door.

"Well, then!"

She throws out a broom and quickly closes her door. Jesse and Matthew look at each other, not sure what to do.

"Was that a yes?"

Matthew shrugs his shoulders, makes his way down to the yard and begins raking. Jesse starts sweeping the porch. Aunt Ginny peaks through the blinds just enough for them to see a sliver of her face and one of her eyes watching the activity. Impishly, she smiles.

Inside the Martinez home, the beautiful scent of holiday baking fills the air. Diann and Harper spread the makings for granola bars onto a cookie sheet and put them in the oven. They make cucumber with cream cheese and chicken salad tea sandwiches and wrap them just so. On the stove is a pot of hot cocoa being warmed. They pour it into a thermos and pack it all in a picnic basket.

A black Mercedes pulls up to the curb at Aunt Ginny's and Sam gets out. He stops and speaks to Matthew and Jesse who are hard at work on the leaf removal.

"Hi guys, looks like you've got quite an undertaking there. That's a lot of leaves!"

Matthew takes a breather and responds.

"Yes sir."

"I hope my aunt is paying you well."

Jesse can't believe his ears. Aunt Ginny has a relative!

"Aunt Ginny is really your aunt?"

"She really is. And like I said, I hope she's paying you well."

Matthew sets the record straight.

"No sir. We're doing this as an act of kindness."

"Well, I'm sure she appreciates it."

Matthew hesitates but then spills the beans.

"We don't know if she does or not. She goes to our church so we've seen her there, but here we've mostly only seen half her face talking to us through a cracked door or one eye staring at us through the blinds."

Sam laughs.

"Well, she's a big tease. But, she has been a little more to herself since her husband, Colonel Pennington, passed away."

Matthew and Jesse are both completely blown away with the new information. Wanting to be certain he heard correctly Matthew revisits the question.

"Her husband was a Colonel?"

Sam smiles and nods affirmatively. Jesse chimes in.

Wow, that's really cool!

"Our dad is a Captain! He's in Afghanistan but he'll be home for Christmas," adds Matthew.

Touched by their obvious pride in their dad and their moving anticipation for him to come home, Sam responds.

"That's great, guys!"

Diann and Harper exit their house with Janee's picnic in tow. They walk toward the boys and Sam standing in Aunt Ginny's yard. Matthew points to Diann and Harper and identifies them to Sam.

"That's our mom and sister."

As Diann and Harper approach, Sam extends his hand to Diann.

"Hi, I'm Sam. Just dropped by for a quick visit with my Aunt Ginny."

Diann shakes his hand and Harper waves at him.

"Hi, Sam. We've actually met before. I'm one of the ministers at Midtown Church. Of course we know Callie,

Pastor Jack and Megan. And, I met you when Becca was in the hospital. We miss her terribly. She was one of a kind."

"She was indeed."

Sam recognizes Harper from the school playground and addresses her.

"Your brothers told me your dad's a soldier."

Harper nods affirmatively.

"Well, that makes him a hero you know. You should be very proud!"

Harper beams as Diann makes introductions.

"This is Harper and I guess you've meet Matthew and Jesse. Boys, we're taking Janee lunch at the hospital so she can sit in the park across the street and have a break. We're going to stay with Mr. Williams for an hour or so."

"Janee at Midtown hospital whose husband has cancer?"

"Yes. Do you know her?"

"I met her yesterday. Actually, I re-met her yesterday. She knew Becca, too. We ran into each other in the lobby. Literally, ran into each other as she got off the elevator."

Diann laughs.

"She drives the school bus for a lot of kids we know and she and her husband go to our church. She's a great asset. She volunteers for every thing! Her husband has really been sick. But, she always has a smile on her face."

Jesse quickly gets his mom up to speed on a fact he thinks she may not be aware of.

"Mom, Aunt Ginny's husband was a Colonel!

Aunt Ginny peaks out the window at the activity.

"Yes honey, she told me that."

Matthew seems astounded at his mom's lack of sharing such important news.

"Really? You got to talk to her? Here at her house or at church?

"Both, honey."

Equally surprised, Jesse wants more details.

"When?"

"We've had tea a few times and at church I speak with her all the time."

The boys seem completely surprised as Diann addresses Sam.

"Well, nice to see you again, Sam. You should think about coming to church sometime. Megan's in the Christmas play. She's quite the little performer! Merry Christmas."

"Merry Christmas. I hope the Captain gets to come home soon."

"Thank you. We hope so, too. Boys, behave! And I mean it! When you finish, stay inside the house and do your homework until we get back. We have to be at church for rehearsal at two o'clock so be changed and ready to go."

Diann and Harper make their way over to Bertha. Diann places the picnic in the backseat next to Harper and gets inside the car. Diann and Harper pray before trying to start the car. Without understanding why, Sam looks on as Matthew and Jesse look at each other, then stand like statues watching their mom as she tries to start Bertha. At first Bertha makes clicking sounds without turning over. Then she sputters and continues struggling to turn over.

Matthew and Jesse cross their fingers hoping the SUV will start. Sam and SSV observe as Matthew and Jesse begin to chant in unison.

"Cmon' Bertha. Cmon."

Aunt Ginny peeks through her blinds at the struggling SUV and crosses her fingers. Finally, the SUV starts.

Diann and Harper cheer with great glee as they begin making their way down the driveway. Aunt Ginny smiles, lifts her hands toward heaven and does a slow twirl, her version of a happy dance. SSV smiles and gives a thumbs-up. Sam takes in the apparent ritual as the boys give each other a high-five and celebrate Bertha's engine starting.

"Yes!"

Sam makes his way onto the porch and knocks on the front door. Aunt Ginny cracks the front door and Sam peeks in through the crack. The boys rake and watch the interaction.

"Aunt Ginny, it's Sam. I can't come in through the crack. Can you open the door a little wider?"

Aunt Ginny quietly laughs to herself.

"Sam who? I used to have a nephew named Sam but his last visit was years ago. I thought he'd been abducted by aliens."

Jesse and Matthew look at each other wide-eyed. Matthew whispers to Jesse.

"Did you hear that? She believes in extraterrestrials?"

Matthew shakes his head.

Sam continues to debate with Aunt Ginny.

"OK, OK, but I'm here now. Better late than never, right? Now open the door!"

"Where are your manners?"

"Open the door, please?"

She opens the door wider but hides behind it out of sight and giggling.

The boys stare at Sam contorting his body to squeeze through. Sam enters by turning side ways and squeezing in. As the door closes the boys shake their heads and go back to raking.

Saturday is always a busy day at Midtown Hospital. But, Janee never notices. For her it's just another day, another chance to be with her beloved husband. Janee sits in a chair beside Rich's bed and knits. A table next to her hosts several books including the Bible. Occasionally, she looks up at Rich sleeping. She stops, lays down her knitting, stands and stretches. She takes a closer look at Rich and pulls his covers up and carefully tucks them beneath his chin. She picks up her Bible, sits back down and begins to read.

There's a light knock on the door. Diann and Harper enter carrying the picnic basket. Janee stands to greet them and they all hug.

"Hi girls! Something smells great!"

"Mama and I made you a picnic!"

"We thought we'd sit here a while with Rich and let you take your picnic across the street to the park and take a little well-deserved break."

Janee smiles and becomes a little emotional as she takes the picnic basket.

"That is so thoughtful. Some non-hospital food and a change of scenery would be nice. Thank you."

"It's an act of kindness!" Harper exclaims.

"Yes, it is, baby!"

Janee smiles and quietly walks out of the room for her well-deserved break.

Now successfully inside her house, Sam and Aunt Ginny sit together in her living room. Aunt Ginny is dressed in a 1940's dress, nail polish and makeup flawlessly applied, vintage jewelry, black pumps and with her silver hair up in a bun.

The interior of her home looks like a museum missing the red velvet ropes. Her furniture is classic, priceless period pieces collected from travels around the world. A small table-top Christmas tree rests on a Chinese game table. She and Sam sit on a Queen Anne couch, sipping their tea. Sam takes a Christmas card out of his breast pocket and hands it to her.

"Usually, Marianna brings by my Christmas gift."

"Well, I just thought I'd like to do it this year. I'm on my way to pick her up. She's coming with me to drop of a donation check to the church."

"Well, good, Sam. I'm happy that you and Callie are on good terms again."

"Well, actually it will be the first time I've seen her since, well, our falling out."

"Oh, so Marianna is your security blanket? Marianna is lovely, you know. And, single, I might add!"

SSV sitting in between them with his arms around the back of couch nods and smiles.

"Yes, Marianna is lovely. I'm just going to try and make things right again with Callie."

"Well, I hope it all works out. Life is short, you know. And wasting time is foolish. Shall I open my card?"

"Please."

"In my honor you have made a donation to Wounded Warriors. Perfect. Thank you, Sam. I couldn't hope for a nicer Christmas gift. Tell me, Sam, where have you been all this time?"

"I've been grieving and in pain and only thinking about myself."

SSV listens with compassion and comments.

"That's a big realization, Sam! Really big!"

Sam jumps and then sighs with frustration. It startles Aunt Ginny.

"Are you ok?"

"Yes, I'm fine. I was just startled."

Aunt Ginny looks around.

"By what? The tea leaves?"

"Ah, no I just thought I heard something."

"Voices in your head? I have that sometimes."

Sam elects not to try and explain. He sets his tea cup and saucer on the coffee table.

"Well, I guess I'd better get going."

They stand and hug each other good-bye.

"Well, tell Marianna hello and give Callie, Jack and Megan my love."

"You know about Megan?"

Aunt Ginny smiles.

"Of course I know about Megan. Everybody knows about Megan!"

"Everybody but me."

"Well, Sam, you know about her now. She lights up any room she enters! And you would have known about her sooner if you hadn't been such a stubborn old mule. Make it right, Sam. It can be fixed."

"Wish me luck. I'm going to invite Callie, Jack and Megan to come to the house for Christmas dinner when Robert and his family come to town. I'd like for you to come, too."

A look of complete panic comes over Aunt Ginny's face.

"Sam, what's come over you?

"What do you mean?"

"Is it terminal? Have you been diagnosed with deadly disease? How long do you have left?"

Sam laughs.

"No, I'm fine. I just want the family to all be together."

"Well, good then! As it should be."

Matthew and Jesse have made several large piles of leaves and are in the process of bagging them up. As Sam exits the front door, he drags Aunt Ginny out with him.

"Look guys, here she is. The mystery is revealed. See, perfectly harmless."

She laughs and struggles to break free of Sam's grip. The boys look her over and wave.

"Boys, you look cold. Would you like some hot cocoa?"

They smile and enthusiastically nod, "yes." SSV is laying in a pile of leaves. Sam notices him as he passes the pile. SSV gives Sam some unsolicited intel.

"When you pick up Marianna, remember that you can get to the church driving right by the hospital."

Sam salutes a large pile of leaves. Aunt Ginny observes from the front porch and mumbles to herself.

"He just saluted a pile of leaves! Must be hearing those voices again. Lord, help him! "

She shakes her head, starts back inside and with her back to them, lifts up her hands and motions the boys toward the front door.

"Boys, come on inside and have some hot cocoa."

The boys comply. They sit at the kitchen table looking all around for any clues that might fuel their curiosity as Aunt Ginny serves them each a mug of hot cocoa. She turns to retrieve two more mugs and places one in front of an empty chair.

"There you go, Colonel. I know how much you love a good mug of cocoa."

The boys are wide-eyed. She sits down with them and begins shuffling a deck of cards. Having no idea what to expect next, they scrutinize her every move.

"You boys were so nice to do an act of kindness for me, now I'm going to return the favor."

Jesse tries to discourage the notion.

"Oh, that's ok, Aunt Ginny, we—"

She interrupts.

"I'm going to teach you how to play Bridge. Keeps you mentally sharp! It's a good game to know."

Matthew attempts to engage with her.

"Our mom plays Bridge. Don't we need four players for that?"

"We have four players. The Colonel will play with us."

Slightly scared, the boys look at each other and stand. Matthew takes charge and has never been so excited to obey his mother by heading next door to do his homework.

"Well, Aunt Ginny, our mom told us when we finished raking to go inside and do our homework until she picks us up for rehearsal at church."

"We better come back another time."

"Ok, then. Just remember, the offer stands. Just the four of us!"

Another idea occurs to Matthew. He decides to test the water.

"Maybe we could bring our mom along to be the fourth player?"

"What do you have against the Colonel? That would hurt his feelings! Why would you want to leave him out like that?"

"I meant no disrespect, Aunt Ginny. It's just that our mom really likes to play Bridge and I thought it might be fun for her."

Jesse decides to bring up another valid point.

"Yeah, plus she's actually alive!"

Diann and Harper sit quietly reading and watching over Rich as medical attendants come in and out of his room checking monitors and changing out his IV bags.

Janee sits on a park bench and peacefully enjoys eating her picnic as she takes in the beauty of the day, letting the sunshine bathe her face. She throws crumbs to a pigeon or two before noticing a homeless person near by going through the trash.

She stands and takes a couple of the sandwiches from her picnic basket, walks over, smiles and extends her hand to offer the food to her. The homeless woman barely looks up at her, but timidly takes the sandwiches and thanks her. Janee goes back to her bench, sits down, takes one long and final gaze at the beauty of the day, then stands and slowly walks back toward the hospital.

Chapter 8

With Christmas music resounding in his car, Sam drives to pick up Marianna. She lives in a lovely, suburban, Craftsman home, festively decorated for Christmas. The interior décor resembles a friendly beach cottage. A white baby grand occupies one corner of the living room. A small misshapen Charlie Brown tree decorated with Charlie Brown ornaments sits on top of a small round table. Dressed in a festive red sweater and jeans, Marianna adds water to the tree stand, adjusts one of the ornaments, then sits at the piano and sings, "Silent Night" as she awaits Sam's arrival.

Marianna hears Sam's Mercedes pull up out front and exits her house, making her way toward the car. Sam gets out to open the passenger side door for her. SSV sits in the backseat. As they make their way through the city streets, Sam and Marianna chat without pause as though they are being reunited after a long separation. SSV looks pleased. They approach the vicinity of the hospital where Diann stands on the side of the road in front of her broken down SUV. Harper looks out the window from inside. Marianna is first to see her.

"That's Diann! She's the music and childhood education minister at our church."

"I know. I re-met her this morning—her and her kids. They live next door to Aunt Ginny."

"That's right. I'd forgotten about that."

Sam and Marianna pull up behind them and exit the car. Marianna waves to Harper and hugs Diann.

"Girl, this car has been letting you down a lot lately."

The AAA tow truck arrives. Diann helps Harper out of the car. The AAA driver opens the hood and investigates.

"You need a new battery, ma'am."

"Can't you just jump it?"

"Not a chance. It's old, tired and dead. We'll have to tow it to the dealership."

Sam takes out a twenty dollar bill to tip the AAA driver and gives him instructions.

"Have them put in a new battery. We'll pick it up later."

"Oh, Sam, thank you. That isn't necessary, really."

"Yes it is, really. Come on. Let's get you some temporary wheels."

Diann and Harper get into Sam's car. SSV is seated between Diann and Harper in the back seat and they drive away. SSV never misses an opportunity for a verbal affirmation.

"Good job, Sam!"

Without expression, Sam looks in the rearview mirror and winks. Thinking the wink belongs to her, Harper winks back.

As they pull down the long drive of the Waters estate, Sam pulls around the back of the house to his eight-car garage. Pointing out all of her options, he offers Diann the choice of whatever she'd like to drive. She chooses a red 1965 Mustang. Sam backs it out for her. She and Harper get in and drive away to pick up the boys.

Diann pulls up into her driveway in forward motion for a change, and honks the horn. Jesse and Matthew come running out and give the car a complete walk around admiring how cool it is. They get in and Diann backs down the drive.

Midtown Church is buzzing today. A number of cars are in the parking lot. After taking several detours to stall as long as possible, Sam and Marianna pull up to the church. SSV, very pleased with the events that are about to unfold, sits in the backseat. Sam stares straight ahead, semi-frozen, making one last effort to postpone this long overdue reunion. Marianna gently touches his hand and reassures him.

"It's time, Sam. You can do this."

A dozen people assemble the sets and props for the Christmas pageant including Diann, Matthew, Jesse, Janee, Jack and Callie. Megan has her wheel chair pulled up to the piano. She and Harper are playing and singing, "Hark! The Herald Angels Sing."

As the squeaky double doors at the rear of the auditorium open, Sam and Marianna walk through them and enter the sanctuary. The high-pitched noise draws everyone's attention. Janee, Diann and her children wave to Sam and Marianna.

Callie recognizes her dad. She stares in disbelief. A few steps in, Sam freezes. Jack and Marianna try reading the faces of Callie and Sam. Everyone else goes back to what they were doing.

Callie's eyes fill with tears as she continues to stare at the father she hasn't seen or heard from in years. She begins to tremble. Jack moves closer to her. SSV sits on the edge of a pew and is turned facing the center aisle watching the two like a tennis match. SSV serves as a cheerleader.

"Don't stop now, Sam. Keep moving."

Hesitantly and with Marianna at his side, Sam slowly continues walking down the aisle. Suddenly, Callie breaks into a dead run toward Sam. She falls into his arms weeping. Marianna cries tears of joy and looks back and forth between the two of them and Jack. Sam holds Callie tightly as tears stream down his face.

"Can you ever forgive me for being such a stubborn fool—for staying away for so long?"

Still crying uncontrollably, Callie nods "yes," before looking up at Sam.

"Yes, Daddy, I forgive you. I'm just happy you're here now. I've played this moment over and over in my head a million times."

As they continue to hug, Jack approaches. Sam extends his hand.

"Jack, I know there are no words to fix what I've done. But, if given the chance, I'll spend the rest of my life trying to make up for all the pain I've caused. I'm sincerely sorry. I hope in time you can forgive me."

"We've already forgiven you. Welcome back, Mr. Waters."

"Sam. Please call me, Sam. Or, Dad if you like."

Jack shakes Sam's hand and Sam pats him on the back. Megan, interrupted by all of the commotion, notices all of the emotional interaction and wheels her rickety wheel chair toward the action. She reaches out for a hug from Marianna who smiles, bends down and complies. Callie and Jack move aside and Sam bends down to her eye level. Megan shares an observation.

"I remember you. I gave you half my sandwich. Except you've had a bath. You look much better now! My name's Megan."

Sam chuckles, then responds.

"My name is Sam."

"Sam is my daddy, honey."

"Well, where have you been? Were you on a long trip of something? If you're my Mommy's dad then that means you are my grandfather?"

"Yes, that's right."

"Well, what do I call you?"

"You decide and let me know."

"OK, I have to think about it. There are a lot of names for grandfathers, you know. Let me see. How about Papa?"

"Papa it is. And what shall I call you?"

"Princess. Or, Princess Megan. Or, just plain Megan."

Sam chuckles.

"Well, fine then."

Marianna winks at Jack, hugs Callie and wipes her tears. Sam smiles, stands, pulls out the check, hands it to Callie and explains his decision to deliver it.

"Wanted to bring this by myself. I know your mother or Marianna have always made a donation to whatever church you are involved with. But, I will be doing it from now on."

"Thank you, Daddy. This always helps our church so much."

Callie hugs him again as Jack explains what's going on.

"We're setting up for our Christmas program. We have a rehearsal this afternoon."

Callie extends the invitation.

"Would you like to stay and watch?"

Looking at Marianna who nods affirmatively.

"I would."

Chapter 9

The church stage looks like old town Bethlehem and dress rehearsal is in full swing. Diann holds a script and blocks all of the scenes for the children. Callie sits at the piano going over some of the songs. The children playing Mary, Joseph and a baby doll Jesus, are all standing in their places to the rear of the stage. Matthew, dressed as an angel, takes center stage and speaks to several shepherds tending their sheep. The shepherds look frightened.

"Fear not, for behold, I bring you good tidings of great joy, which shall be to all people. For unto you is born this day in the city of David a Savior, which is Christ the Lord. And this shall be a sign unto you: You shall find the babe wrapped in swaddling clothes, lying in a manger."

The combined children's and adult choir sing, "King Jesus is His Name," with Janee singing the solo part. At the conclusion, Harper and Megan, along with several other children dressed as angels, gather around Jesse. Jesse, dressed in Biblical garb, continues the narrative. Diann gives him the go ahead.

"Suddenly, a great company of heavenly hosts appeared with the angel praising God and saying—"

Harper, Megan and a number of other children join in.

"Glory to God in the highest and on earth peace, good will toward men."

Sam and Marianna watch and smile. SSV sits in the pew beside them proudly observing the heart-felt performance. The shepherds, wisemen and magistrate bow before Mary, Joseph and baby Jesus, bringing Him gifts and worshipping Him as the choir, composed of adults and children and conducted by Diann, sing, "Oh, Come All Ye Faithful."

At the conclusion of the song, Jack invites the congregation to sing along for one final song.

"And now please all stand and sing together with us, 'Joy to the World.'"

Sam, Marianna and SSV stand and sing along. At the conclusion, Diann makes some house- cleaning announcements.

"Great job everybody! I think we're ready!"

Janee approaches Diann and whispers in her ear. Megan and Harper join Sam and Marianna as Diann continues.

"Everyone, for years Janee and her husband, Rich have played Santa and Mrs. Claus when we deliver gifts to the Bethany Home for Children. This year, Rich is in the hospital and not able to be Santa. Janee needs to take care of him and won't be able to be with us this year."

Janee solicits their replacements.

"So who's going to volunteer to take our places?"

Everyone looks around and at each other but with no response. Marianna raises her hand. SSV smiles, leans over and whispers in Sam's ear.

"She's really good for you, Sam."

Diann acknowledges her.

"Yes, Marianna?"

"Sam and I will do it!"

Sam can't believe what she just volunteered him to do. Callie and Jack look at each other and smile. Megan leans over to Harper and proudly brags on her grandfather.

"He's my Papa!"

Callie raises her hand to get Diann's attention and makes an announcement.

"Yes, Callie?"

"All next week is our TAG Love campaign. Remember you are representing God and His love and honoring Him by giving and serving others."

Jack underscores her reminder.

"Have fun and bless as many people as you can!"

Callie walks toward Sam, Marianna, Megan and Harper as Sam asks her for further clarification.

"What's Tag Love?"

"It's actually something Mama started. We tag people by doing random acts of kindness to demonstrate God's love and then tell the recipient to pass it on. Would you like to come along with us?"

Sam is hesitant. Marianna looks at Sam and nods, "Yes." Jack approaches as Megan makes her desires known.

"Yeah, Papa, come with us for Tag Love! Tell him, Marianna!"

Marianna teases Sam as she echoes Megan's wishes.

"Yeah, Papa!"

Unable to resist Jack joins in the fun.

"Yeah, Papa!"

"Come on, Papa!" says SSV.

Obviously outnumbered, Sam may as well wave a white flag indicating his willingness to surrender.

"OK, Papa's in! Just tell me where and when."

Everyone enjoys the sparring and is sensing a lot of joy, laughter and bonding. SSV approaches Sam.

"You did good, Sam. Real good. You're really connecting the dots."

Sam smiles, nods and joins Marianna as she mingles with the others and says goodbye to Janee, Callie, Jack and Megan. Sam moves closer to Diann.

"How about we follow you to the dealership to pick up your car?"

Sam makes sure Diann's SUV has a new battery and pays for it. He checks to make sure it's in good shape to get them home safely. Marianna drives the Mustang and Sam follows her back to the Waters Estate. They make their way down the long drive and around the back of the house to park in the eight-car garage. As they exit the garage, Sam has a suggestion.

"How do you feel about a ride by the lake at sunset?"

"I'd like that."

Together they walk to the stables and saddle up two beautiful stallions, then lead them out of the stables and through the gate. They mount them and ride off across the pasture, galloping across a vast acreage of winter grass surrounded by mature, bare trees that are dark and lacy under the late afternoon sky.

Reaching the lake, they dismount. Holding the reins of their horses they walk and talk while making their way around this scenic setting. The final hour of sunshine reflects off the water as the horses pause to drink. SSV skips a rock across the still, glass-like lake. The growing sunset painted in hues of peach, orange and purple is stunning. They remount and begin making their way back to the house. They put away the saddles, cool down the horses, feed them and then go inside to get warm and have something to eat.

They find comfortable seats in the family room's high-back chairs. In the light of the Christmas tree, Sam and Marianna enjoy chatting, laughing and tasting appetizers of brie, grapes, carved chateaubriand, French bread and wine. Secretly, neither is ready for the night to end. But, soon, it's that time.

Sam drives Marianna home. SSV sits in the back seat. Sam watches him in the rearview mirror as Marianna recounts the earlier activities of the day.

"I don't think your reconciliation with Callie and Jack, or meeting Megan, could have gone any better, do you?"

"It did go well. I'm grateful they walk the talk."

"Walk the talk?"

"Forgiveness. They live what they espouse."

"Yes, they do. I've never known them to be any other way."

"Callie's always adored you."

"She's the daughter I never had. And what did you think about that precocious, adorable little granddaughter of yours?"

"She's really something, isn't she?"

"She is quite the character! Keeps us all on our toes!"

"The two of you seem to be close, too."

"I'm her babysitter on date night! And sometimes she just likes to come over for a visit. I think it has to do with my baby grand. She loves to play the piano."

SSV has remained mute for as long as he can and offers some direction.

"She's a beautiful woman, Sam. Ever thought about asking her on a real date. Or are you happy with continuing spending every waking moment together without defining it?"

Sam looks in the rear view mirror at SSV and gives him a look. As usual, SSV is unfazed.

"Just sayin'!"

Sam pulls up out front of Marianna's house. He opens her car door and walks her to the door.

"I'll see you tomorrow."

"Good night, Sam."

She starts to go in just as he turns back around and stops her.

"Marianna, wait."

Sam walks back up to the porch.

"Thank you for being there with me, today. It meant a lot."

"It was my pleasure. I'm actually happy that I got to personally witness the reunion."

Sam starts to walk away again. Marianna starts to go inside. Sam stops her again.

"Marianna?"

Since they've known each other for over thirty years, she finds humor in Sam's seeming awkwardness and quietly laughs as she turns around again. Sam walks back up onto the porch.

"Would you ever want to maybe go out—like on an actual, official date?"

Very pleased with the idea, she smiles and responds.

"I would like that very much."

"Good!"

Sam gives her a nervously executed hug and leaves. She smiles as she watches him walk toward his car before going inside. SSV, with his arm around Sam's shoulder playfully walks beside him. From Marianna's vantage point, Sam looks like he's having trouble keeping his balance. Marianna goes inside as Sam and SSV, who is now riding shotgun, drive away.

Smiling broadly, Marianna plugs in the festive lights and plops down in front of her Charlie Brown tree. After a brief pause, she stands, goes to the piano and begins playing and singing, "This Christmas."

Continuing to make their way home, Sam smiles broadly and turns up the radio that is playing, "This Christmas." SSV, happily smiling and very content with the day's events, keeps time to the song with his head jogging side to side.

Chapter 10

It's noon and a beautiful crisp, cool Sunday in Atlanta. Jack and Callie stand at the doors of Midtown Church shaking hands and telling everyone goodbye as the congregation exits the church.

Thirty or so congregants gather in the fellowship hall where on this day it has become an annual tradition for soup and bread to be served for lunch. Sam and Marianna, dressed as Santa and Mrs. Claus, and Megan, dressed as an elf, sit together awaiting their soup. Aunt Ginny, wearing all white with a halo and angel wings springing out from her back joins them, along with Diann, Matthew, Jesse and Harper, also dressed as elves. SSV stands against the wall drinking in the activity.

Callie and Jack enter the fellowship hall and laugh when they see Santa, Mrs. Claus, the angel and the elves all awaiting lunch. Jack addresses everyone.

"Thank you all for joining us for our soup and bread lunch. We asked that everyone donate the amount of money you'd have spent going out to lunch. All of the money collected will go to the Food Bank that helps, all year long, individuals and families who've fallen on hard times."

Callie adds her comments.

"And remember that this delicious meal of soup and bread is more than 90% of the people in the world will have to eat today. Let's thank Janee for making it for us."

Wearing her apron, Janee, enters and takes a bow as everyone gives her a standing ovation. Jack says grace.

"Let's bow our heads and bless our food. Heavenly Father, we are so grateful for this day and your many blessings toward us, including this delicious lunch. Be with those who are not as fortunate. Keep our eyes, ears and hearts opened to make a difference."

Sam has heard that line before, opens his eyes and looks around for SSV. SSV stands beside Jack. He winks at Sam and Sam goes back to bowing his head in prayer.

"Use this food to nourish our bodies that we might serve you with our whole heart. And be with us as we deliver gifts to Bethany Children's home. Let the children feel your love through us. In Jesus' name I pray these things, Amen."

After enjoying their soup and bread, everyone excitedly makes their way to Bethany Children's Home.

Upon entering the home, they all walk down a long, wide hallway and into a large playroom modestly decorated for Christmas. There are about twenty children ages five to twelve.

Sam and Marianna sit at the front of the room in their Santa and Mrs. Claus outfits. The younger children crowd around Sam and a couple of them try to jump up in his lap. He is cheerful and very accommodating. Others talk to Marianna.

Aunt Ginny floats around in her angel outfit smiling at everyone and passing out five-dollar bills. The elves pass out the gifts and stockings to the children. As they begin to open them, their faces light up like the noonday sun.

Santa and Mrs. Claus pass out Christmas cookies and candy canes. The elves, Jack and Callie serve hot chocolate and marshmallows in paper cups with lids. At the close of the program, Harper and Megan sing, "Noel." Some of the children, Santa, Mrs. Claus, Aunt Ginny, Jack, Callie, Diann, Matthew and Jesse sing along. SSV approvingly observes all of the joy as the festivities come to a close. The children wave and blow kisses as the church group exits.

Still in full Santa and Mrs. Santa attire, Sam and Marianna drive away singing along to, "It Came Upon a Midnight Clear" as it plays on the radio. SSV sits in the backseat keeping time by rocking his head back and forth. Sam poses a question.

"Are you ready for our first date?"

"Sure, what'd you have in mind?"

Without changing clothes, they pull up to the Cherokee Country Club, an exclusive, members-only club. The valet greets them and they go inside.

The dining room is beautifully decorated with elegant, antique holiday fare. The wait staff is in white starched shirts, black vests and black bow ties. Dinners are being served on fine china under sterling plate covers. Crystal glasses and stemware with silver flatware are perfectly placed on linen tablecloths. The maitre d', who knows Sam well, is slightly taken back by their costumes. He greets Sam with a friendly handshake and leads them to their table.

A waiter fills their water glasses as Sam and Marianna peruse the menu. Patrons throughout the dining room stare, whisper, laugh and talk about the presence of Santa and Mrs. Claus live and up close. A few children dining with their families enthusiastically wave at them. Sam and Marianna smile and wink back at their following as their waiter returns to take their order.

In very short order, their courses are served with slow-paced, methodical delivery. First, the waiter opens a bottle of Pouilly Fuisse and pours a sample for Sam. With his nod of approval he pours Marianna a glass and then fills Sam's.

They toast and have a sip. Both find it amazing that after all these years of knowing one another, they seem to have discovered so much in common and so much to talk about. SSV, hovering around the musicians, couldn't be more pleased.

The waiter returns to make eggless Caesar salads tableside—first the organic oil, fresh squeezed lemon juice, shaved Parmesan and then the chopped anchovies. Sam asks Mrs. Claus a very important question.

"Are you a fan of anchovies?"

"Love anchovies!"

Sam makes a request of the waiter.

"Could you give us extra anchovies?"

The waiter happily complies then adds in the Romaine lettuce and homemade croutons. He tosses and serves equal portions on chilled plates.

Sam and Marianna enjoy the salad and continue what seems to be a never-ending, very enjoyable conversation.

The waiter revisits the table to clear the salad plates and deliver the entrée. Steak and lobster, asparagus with Hollandaise and baked potatoes with butter, sour cream and chives is served. After the main course is consumed, their dinner is concluded with two cups of espresso served in demitasse cups.

Although a string ensemble has been playing the entire time, they pause their conversation just long enough to notice. Sam stands, bows and extends his hand to Marianna for a dance. She smiles and complies. They dance to several vintage Christmas songs.

Sam spots a photographer and calls him over. The photographer takes several shots of them posing as they dance. They laugh and continue talking and dancing until the ensemble takes a break. Regretfully, they decide to call it a night.

As Sam and Marianna exit the club, it is pointed out to them by others awaiting their cars, that they are standing underneath mistletoe. They look slightly uncomfortable, but then Sam gently kisses her on the cheek. They look at each other for a long pause and then share a sweet first kiss. Several children cover their eyes in disbelief as other patrons waiting on their cars applaud. Sam and Marianna laugh and take a bow.

Over at the Martinez house, everyone is dressed in pajamas and ready for bed. Diann, Jesse, Matthew and Harper huddle before an iPad talking with Harry as he tries to get an overview of the day's events.

"What did you do today?"

"We went to church and it was a wonderful service," says Diann.

Harper chimes in.

"And, then we went to give out presents at the children's home."

Jesse adds his two cents.

"Mom made us dress up as elves!"

Matthew punctuates the drama.

"Yeah, it was so embarrassing!"

Harry offers some fatherly advice.

"Well guys, don't ever let doing something special for those who are less fortunate embarrass you. I'm proud of you for helping your mom like that."

"And guess what, Daddy. My friend, Megan's Papa, dressed up like Santa! Maybe next year, you can play Santa," Harper suggests.

"Maybe I can, Harper."

"We are counting the days until you come home, honey," says Diann.

"Me, too! Well, I gotta get to work. You kids take care of Mama, and I'll see you soon."

"We love you, honey!"

In unison and on cue the kids respond.

"We love you, Daddy!"

"I love you, too."

The screen goes black.

Across town in a modest suburban home, Jack and Callie are finishing phase one of tucking in Megan as Callie reads her a bedtime story from a Christmas storybook.

"There are many gifts at Christmas that can last the whole year through. But, there's one gift that lasts forever. And, Jesus, that gift is You!"

Callie closes the book and Jack pulls up her covers.

"OK, princess Megan, it's time to say your prayers and go to sleep."

"But, I'm not tired, Daddy."

Callie reminds Megan what tomorrow is.

"Tomorrow we have to be up very early for Tag Love. So it's time to go to sleep."

Now, resigned, Megan settles down and folds her hands to pray.

"OK. Dear God, thank you for Mommie and Daddy. Thank you for my Papa and Marianna and all of my family. Help the people in the world who are hungry or lonely to get food and friends. And tell Jesus, 'Hi.' Amen."

"Good prayer, Megan," Jack says proudly.

"We love you, sweet girl."

"Love you, more!"

Jack and Callie respond in unison.

"No way!"

Jack and Callie kiss her good night and turn off her lights. She's asleep before they exit her room.

Chapter 11

The peach and yellow hues of sunrise are brushed like watercolors across the early morning sky. Today is Tag Love Day! Tag Love has become a church tradition that has not only caught on with the Midtown Church congregation, but has begun spreading throughout the community.

Barely able to sleep because of the excitement and anticipation, Diann and the kids are up extra early. Even so, they still seem to always be running slightly behind. They race out of the house and get into the SUV parked facing the street. Diann struggles to get Bertha started. Finally she starts. Diann looks down at the gas gage, realizing she's on empty.

"Oh, no!"

As she coasts down the driveway, Jesse inquires.

"What's wrong, Mama?"

"I forgot we need gas. We're on empty. And we're already running late. Oh well, we have no choice but to stop for gas."

Across town, Jack, Callie, Marianna, Sam, Megan and SSV, all loaded into Jack's van, pull up to order at the drive thru at Chick-fil-A. Renee, an employee in her late teens, takes their order as Jack belts it out.

"We need a dozen chicken biscuits. And we want to pay for the person's order behind us. Just tell them Merry Christmas, God loves them and pass it on. It's called Tag Love."

"Will do!" Renee says cheerfully.

Jack pulls up, pays and is handed the biscuits. Then, he hands Renee a ten-dollar bill.

"And that's for you! Merry Christmas, God loves you and pass it on!"

"Wow! Thank you!"

Jack smiles and slowly pulls away as everyone turns around to see the expression on the face of the driver in the car behind them. As the car approaches to pay, Renee delivers the news.

"Good morning. Your order's been paid for. Merry Christmas, God loves you and pass it on!"

The expression on the driver face is priceless. He expresses gratitude.

"Muchas gracias! Dios te bendiga! Feliz Navidad!"

Everyone enjoys getting to see the reaction. Jack pulls away and onto the main highway toward Starbucks. Once there, Jack pulls up to the drive thru and orders from an older gentleman wearing a reindeer hat. Callie, Marianna, Sam, Megan and SSV watch and listen.

"We'll have a dozen tall hot chocolates with whipped cream and we need those in ride boxes. And we want to pay for the car behind us. Tell them Merry Christmas, God loves them and to pass it on!"

They go through the drive thru window, tip, pay, take their goods and pull away slowly to observe the reaction of the driver behind them. The driver of the car behind them has four people in it. As they are given the news, all four bounce up and down in their seats. Everyone in Jack's car does high fives and smiles with great satisfaction. Sam wants to know what's next.

"Now, where to?"

"You'll see, Papa!"

The van pulls into a gas station and parks in the corner of the parking lot to assess those pulling up at the pumps. Megan addresses Sam.

"You're gonna love this part, Papa!"

Looking for the perfect opportunity, Jack, Callie, Marianna, Megan and SSV scope out the customers as they pull in to get gas. They have hot cocoa and chicken biscuits to give away to just the right vehicle. Megan explains as Sam takes in their strategy.

"See, Papa we just sit here and watch who pulls up for gas. And when we see just the right car—look Mama, that's Miss Diann!"

SSV smiles and nods, pleased with Megan's ability to read a situation.

"She's got a natural instinct for spotting people in need. Do you notice that, Sam?"

Slightly irritated, Sam responds.

"Yes!"

Everyone looks at Sam as he tries to recover.

"Yes, I think you're right, Megan. That is Diann."

SSV can't let a teaching opportunity pass.

"Megan's ears, eyes and heart are always open."

Not able to control his impulse to spar with SSV, Sam blurts out a response.

"I get it! OK, I get it!"

Everyone but Megan seems confused by Sam's comments. Megan pats Sam on the shoulder.

"That's good you get it, Papa. It's your first time."

Diann pulls up to pump #8. She jumps out of the SUV and swipes her credit card. The pump says, "See Attendant." Diann is not unfamiliar with this message.

"Not today! Please, Lord! I'm on fumes!"

Megan makes a declaration that rivals shooting off a starter gun for runners of a marathon!

"Let's Tag Love them, Mama!"

Momentarily, they all continue to observe a frantic Diann as she opens the car door and takes another credit card from her purse. She slides the card and again the pump says, "See Attendant."

Jack, Callie, Megan, Marianna and SSV know the drill and know it's time. Sam is still in training so he will require some coaching. They all stare out the window waiting for just the right moment.

Jesse, Harper and Matthew are out of their seat beats and stare out the car windows at their mom as she desperately attempts to try and get some gas. Completely frustrated, Diann gets back into her van.

"Kids, check on the floor and in between the seats for change."

The kids comply as Diann looks in the ashtray, finds some change and then dumps out her purse on the seat to continue to search. She stuffs what she finds in her coat pocket.

Jack, Callie, Sam, Marianna, Megan and SSV exit the van with such intention they look like they are being deployed. Callie places the bag with biscuits in Megan's lap and wheels her toward Diann's car.

Marianna carries a ride box with hot chocolate. Jack and Sam dart toward Diann's windshield and the gas pump. Suddenly, Tag Love surrounds all the occupants of ole Bertha.

Sam swipes his credit card and begins pumping gas. Jack cleans the windshield. Proudly and with his arms crossed, SSV slowly walks around the car taking in all the activity involved in this lovefest. Marianna and Callie open the doors and with Megan's help pass out biscuits and hot cocoa. Diann sits in the driver's seat stunned that she's been tagged. She begins to laugh and cry simultaneously.

Diann stares at the windshield being cleaned. She turns and sees Sam pumping gas. Jesse passes her a hot cocoa and a biscuit. She continues observing all the blessings being bestowed and tears up again. The kids giggle and eat their treats. Diann rolls down her windows and addresses the gang.

"You have no idea what a blessing this is!"

Sam, Marianna, Callie, Jack and Megan smile and give her and her kids a thumbs-up. SSV leans against the van very pleased with all of the love and care just dispensed. Sam finishes pumping gas, the windshield is clean and everyone's been treated to breakfast.

Sam, Marianna, Jack, Callie and Megan quickly make their way back to their van where SSV is already seated. They drive away enthusiastically waving at Diann and her kids. Everyone is gleeful and sings, "Deck the Halls" as they ride.

Still stunned from being tagged, Diann wipes another tear and blows her nose. Whispering, she says a quiet prayer.

"Thank you, Lord. You are so faithful toward us!"

As "Deck the Halls," concludes, Callie can't contain herself.

"Well, what do you think, Daddy?"

"I think Tag Love is a fantastic idea!"

Jack smiles and underscores the inception of the original concept.

"Remember, it all started as Becca's idea."

"It has her fingerprints all over it! Look, I know this is really last minute, but, I was wondering if all of you might be able to come to the house for an early dinner tonight? I know it's not much notice, but…"

"Can we Mama?"

"Sounds perfect."

Marianna fuels the fire.

"Megan did you know that Papa has horses at his house?"

"Really, Papa? I love horses!"

Marianna continues.

"He has another of your other favorite things at his house, too."

Megan contemplates her best guess.

"A piano?"

Not just any piano, a grand piano," says Marianna.

A grand piano? I've never seen a real one. Am I dreamin'?"

Everyone laughs as Sam suggests an idea.

"Hey, I have an idea who we can Tag Love next! Take a right at the next light."

They park at the Midtown Hospital, and with their biscuits and hot cocoa in tow, make their way up to Rich's room. They knock on the door and quietly enter. Janee reads her Bible and sits beside Rich, still asleep. Jack, Callie, Megan, Sam, Marianna and SSV enter. Janee lights up and stands to greet everyone. Megan hands her two biscuits and Marianna hands her two hot cocoas. SSV takes a seat in the windowsill.

Rich slowly begins to stir. Weakened physically but not in humor, he weighs in.

"Something sure smells good. I know it's not hospital food."

Janee comments.

"Well, since we're going home soon, I guess it won't hurt for you to have a taste."

She opens the biscuit and gives Rich a bite, then a sip of cocoa.

"Delicious! Merry Christmas to me!"

Jack inquires.

"How you feeling, Rich?"

"Not too bad, Rev."

Callie makes the introduction.

"Rich, I don't think you know my Dad, Sam."

"Nice to meet you, Sir."

"You, too Sam."

Unable to contain her enthusiasm, Megan shares more information with Rich.

"He's my Papa! And he has a grand piano and horses at his house!"

Janee can't avoid giving Megan some advice.

"Is that right? Well now, I know you like horses, but you be real careful. You don't want to get hurt again."

"Even though that fall landed her in this chair, she has never waned in her love of horses," says Jack.

"If we'd let her, she'd keep one in her bedroom," says Callie.

Everyone laughs.

"Janee, how elated are you to be taking this fine gentleman home in time for Christmas?" asks Marianna.

SSV proudly observes as Janee smiles.

"I'm thrilled and I thank the good Lord! "

Not to be outdone, Rich offers his sentiments.

"She thinks she's happy?"

"Well, you go back to resting and we'll check back on you soon," says Callie.

"You made my day," says Rich as he takes another sip of cocoa.

"Thank you all for the Tag Love. You definitely made our day!" Janee exclaims.

Everyone smiles, says their goodbyes and then exits back to the van. As they pull out of the parking lot onto the highway, the spirit of Tag Love overtakes Sam.

"I have another idea!"

Everyone listens intently as SSV ribs Sam.

"I think someone's really into Tag Love!"

It's early afternoon as a brand-new blue SUV with a big red bow on it, followed by the van, pulls up into Diann's driveway.

Sam and Marianna get out of the front seat of the SUV and SSV out of the back. They put the keys on top of the driver's front tire as SSV straightens the bow. Marianna holds a note in her hand, places it in an envelop, goes to the front door and tapes the note to the door. The note says, "Merry Christmas, God loves you, pass it on! Keys on top of drivers side tire. Title is in the glove box."

They head back to the van where Jack, Callie and Megan are cheering and giving high-fives. Sam and Marianna enter the van so that Jack can deliver them back to Sam's car.

Megan comments.

"You're the best at Tag Love of anybody I have ever seen, Papa!"

"Thank you, Princess Megan! You are a good teacher!"

Sam smiles at her adoringly. She leans in for a hug. As the van pulls up to drop Sam and Marianna back to Sam's Mercedes, everyone says their goodbyes. Sam reminds them of his last minute invitation.

"See you at the house for dinner."

Now back in Sam's Mercedes, he and Marianna drive to his house. SSV sits in the backseat.

"Marianna, I was wondering if you'd like to help me with plans for Robert and his family's Christmas visit?"

"Of course! Do you know how long they'll be staying?"

Disappointed with the superficial candor of it all, Sam replies, "Their usual drill is only long enough for dinner and presents. Then off to Aspen for their ski week."

"If you know what you'd like to give each of them I'd be happy to shop for your gifts. They sent a list, you know."

"Oh. No, I haven't seen it yet. But, I wanted to do something different this year; something more meaningful. I have a few ideas but wanted you to weigh in."

"What kind of ideas?"

"I'd like to start some new family traditions. For years, Becca begged me to alter our gift-giving habits—to invest in things that really matter. And to teach our children and grandchildren to do the same.

Chapter 12

Sam and Marianna arrive at the Waters Estate, exit the car, go inside and join Francie and Belle sitting at the kitchen table formulating a meal plan for the family visit. Francie reels off her suggested menu.

"I was thinking an appetizer tray with shrimp, crab legs and lobster with cocktail sauce and drawn garlic butter. Then for the main course: turkey, dressing, mashed potatoes, gravy, green beans, broccoli, squash, cranberry sauce, rolls and an assortment of pies for dessert. Is that what you had in mind?"

Belle is the first to weigh in.

"Yum! Sounds scrumptious!"

Sam brings the menu planning to a screeching halt.

"I was thinking soup—soup and bread."

Belle and Francie are taken aback. Marianna listens.

"Just like we had at church on Sunday. When I heard that soup and bread is more than 90% of the world has to eat in a day, it really hit me."

Marianna, Francie and Belle continue listening.

"Robert and his family have always lived a privileged life. Becca always said so and warned me against spoiling the kids. Callie and her family get it. They serve people and sacrifice to give. I think I've done Robert a disservice."

Belle respectfully attempts to convince Sam to teach those who need to be taught and for those who don't, let them be.

"OK, Mr. Sam, Robert needs a lesson, but we don't. Can Francie make that meal for the staff?"

Sam, Marianna and SSV laugh.

"Sure, Belle. You and Francie work out the menu for the staff dinner."

Marianna looks over a printed piece of paper and begins to share its contents with Sam.

"Here is the wish list Robert and Tessa sent over for your gift buying. Shall I read it?"

Sam nods affirmatively as she begins.

"Robert would like a Ferrari in red. That's the only color that will do. And I'm quoting."

"Well, I think we're going to be fresh out of red ones this year."

"Tess wants a trip to Paris and a week long stay at the Peninsula."

Sam responds sarcastically.

"The Peninsula is about $4,000 a night. But, that's a much more reasonable gift than Robert's."

Francie and Belle roll their eyes at each other and smile discreetly.

"Bobby would like his own speed boat so he and his friends can take up parasailing. He'd also like all of the parasailing equipment."

"He's ten!"

Sam, broken-hearted, shakes his head in disbelief.

"Chloe would like cash—a lot of it, she says."

"Cash? And, Chloe's only eight! I think I will do what I can to help these four have a reality check. They've lost all sight of what really matters, much in part to my lack of guidance. I take full blame."

SSV sits on the countertop, listening and tosses out some wisdom.

"Wise, wise decision, Sam. It's never too late to break bad habits and turn things around. Look at you, for instance?"

SSV laughs, teasing Sam. Sam furrows his brow at a counter top. Everyone turns to check out the source of his interaction where nothing is apparent, then look back at Sam.

Over at the Martinez home, Diann and the kids pull up to their drive way. However, just before backing their SUV into position, Diann notices the new SUV. She puts the SUV in park at the curb and everyone jumps out.

Jesse notices the note on the door and they all run toward it. The kids gather round her as Diann reads the note aloud. She begins to weep. The kids jump up and down like they're riding a pogo stick, run back to their new gift and begin examining it inside and out. They quickly retrieve the keys, open the doors and get in. So shocked, overwhelmed and but for occasional squeals completely speechless, they sit silently investigating all of the bells and whistles.

Aunt Ginny stares out her living room window and celebrates right along with them by lifting her hands toward heaven and slowly twirling around in circular fashion.

Now late afternoon, Marianna and Sam stand at the front door to greet them as the Thornsbys pull up and park in the driveway of the Waters Estate.

They escort them into the festively decorated family room where the fireplace is ablaze. Megan is wide-eyed as she examines all of the lights and ornaments on the tree. Belle enters carrying a silver tray with eggnog for the adults and a hot cocoa for Megan. Sam tells Marianna, Jack and Callie to be seated as Belle serves up her goodies.

"We have eggnog for the big people and a hot cocoa for the princess."

Megan notices the grand piano.

"Papa, may I play your grand piano?"

Sam gets up, moves the stool off to the side and sits on it to watch Megan. Megan rolls her chair over and begins to play, "Away in a Manger." At the conclusion, everyone applauds. Megan grins, places her arm across her waist and bows. Then, she poses a question.

"Papa, may I see your horses?"

"Sure you can. But, it'll be dark soon so we need to hurry. Next time come earlier in the day so you can take a ride."

"Really?"

Smiling and assuring her of his offer, Sam picks her up and heads to the stables.

"Really!"

Sam carries Megan and lets her feed pieces of apple to several of the horses. Marianna leads one of the horses over for her to pet. Megan rests her head on the horses neck and hugs him as Callie and Jack watch. SSV sits on top of the fence, happily observing. After a short time and as the sun disappears behind the horizon, the family goes back inside for dinner.

Sam, Marianna, Jack, Callie and Megan enjoy kale salad with apples and gorgonzola, baked chicken with capers and lemon butter garlic sauce, mashed potatoes and broccoli. They all converse, laugh and seem to enjoy each other as though no time has been lost.

Francie brings in an angel food cake, with strawberries, whipped cream and shaved chocolate. Megan is wide-eyed with delight as she is served dessert. Sam asks a few questions to try and get an idea of what everyone would like for Christmas.

"One of the reasons I wanted to have you over is to find out if you could give me a few ideas of what you'd like for Christmas? Megan, you go first."

"Well, I would like to come over and see you more often Papa and play your piano and ride your horses."

"Megan, you can come over as often as you like. But, what else would you like for Christmas?"

"I wish I could take some more piano lessons. And, I really like to read new books! And we saw a really pretty blue winter coat at the store the other day. But, Mama said it costed too much and I can get one more year out of my old one."

Marianna is taking notes.

"Callie and Jack? What would you like for Christmas?"

"Daddy, being here with you is a gift I've prayed for, for years. I feel like I already got my Christmas present."

"Cmon, give me a few hints. You can have as much of this as you want. But, tell me something I can get for you."

Jack jumps in.

"I'll tell you something."

"Don't you dare!"

Jack ignores her.

"She wants to get her hair cut at this swanky place in Buckhead. Only thing is haircuts are seventy dollars and she will not, no matter what, splurge. She also saw a pair of shoes she really likes at a department store. But, instead of getting them, she used the money to buy diapers for a single mom."

Callie gives Jack a look and shakes her head. SSV, seated at the far end of the table, smiles approvingly.

"How about you, Jack?"

"For me it's Christmas every day! I have the best wife in the world and a beautiful daughter. I have everything I need."

Sam smiles approvingly.

"Ok, Marianna, if he's not going to give us a hint, we'll just guess!"

Smiling, Marianna jots down a few thoughts. Sam addresses everyone.

"Robert and his family will be in for a visit next week. I'd like for all of you to come have dinner with us. Aunt Ginny is coming, too."

Marianna comments.

"It will be a surprise for Robert and his family for everyone to be here."

Megan is sleepy, but nonetheless enthusiastic. Yawning, she musters the energy to weigh in.

"I love surprises!"

Callie enthusiastically accepts the invitation.

"We'd love to!"

Cross-eyed tired, Megan gets in one more request.

"Papa may I come over tomorrow and ride a horse?"

"Come over anytime you like, Megan."

"Will you be here too, Miss Marianna?"

Sam and Marianna look at each other and give Megan two simultaneous but different answers.

"Yes/Maybe."

The adults laugh as Megan's eyes close and she falls asleep in her chair.

Over at the Martinez house, Diann and the kids sit at the kitchen table telling Harry about their gas station adventure and the new SUV. Diann continues the conversation.

"We got Tagged not once, but twice today!"

Communicating via iPads, Harry responds.

"A full tank of gas, biscuits and hot cocoa! But, there's more?"

The kids giggle, Diann smiles and they continue talking to Harry. Diann sets the stage.

"We saved the best for last!"

"Well, c'mon, don't keep me in suspense!"

Jesse shares the good news.

"Dad, when we got home today, there was a brand new, blue SUV in our driveway!"

"What? I don't think I heard that right?"

Diann holds up her phone with pictures to confirm the news.

"Look, honey and it came with the keys and the title."

"That is just crazy! Who do you think would do such a thing?"

"Someone who appreciates your service and wants to bless our family."

"That is just incredible. I don't know what to say! Well, what are you going to do with Bertha?"

Matthew discloses the plan.

"We're going to sell her for parts."

Harper punctuates the end of the story.

"Then, we're going to take that money and Tag Love with it!"

"That's a great idea, kids. I'm very proud of you. Have you named the new SUV yet?"

In perfect unison, everyone responds.

"Bertha Junior!"

Chapter 13

It's midmorning at Midtown Hospital and Rich, dressed and sitting in a wheel chair, is about to be released to go home for Christmas. Janee sits beside him holding his hand and talking with him.

A nurse enters and hands release forms on a clipboard and three prescriptions to Janee. She also offers a few instructions.

"Here are your release forms to sign and instructions for taking his meds. He needs to drink plenty of fluids and eat bland foods for a few more days. The prescriptions he takes with meals, three times a day. And the doctor wants to check him in three weeks."

Janee looks over the paperwork and comes to the last page. It's an itemized statement. The total of the bill comes to $705,286. At the bottom, in red, it says, "Balance due zero, paid in full. God loves you, Merry Christmas. Pass it on!"

Janee gasps, places her hand over her heart and stares at the invoice. She looks up at the nurse. The words won't come, only tears. Rich tries comforting her.

"Honey, we already knew what my tab was. There's no need to get upset. We will pay what we can every month. We can only do what we can do."

Wide-eyed, sobbing and still speechless, Janee hands Rich the clipboard. He sees what she sees and starts crying with her.

"Who would have done such a thing?"

Wiping her tears, blowing her nose and with a quivery voice she responds.

"I'm pretty sure I know—thank you, Jesus! Thank you, thank you, thank you!"

Megan awakened very early knowing that Papa had promised her a ride on one of his horses. As they arrive back at the Waters Estate, Marianna leads a saddled Shetland pony out of the stable. Sam lifts Megan from her wheel chair, situates her in the saddle and buckles her in. Marianna and Sam lead her around the ring. Megan talks to the pony, pets him and hugs him. Jack and Callie watch and SSV sits on the fence observing, as well. Sam can't help but remember the words of SSV the first time he laid eyes on this beautiful little granddaughter that he didn't know existed.

"You know, Sam, it's nothing short of a miracle when something that was once lost is found."

Sam lifts Megan from the pony and holds onto her, propped against him and standing while she feeds the pony pieces of an apple. Marianna leads the pony back to the stable. Megan turns with her upper body and hugs Sam around his legs. He lifts her up and carries her to her wheelchair.

Sam pushes Megan while Jack, Callie and Marianna walk along side. They approach the van in the driveway and Megan sees something. As they get closer a surprise is revealed. It's a brand new electric wheel chair. Megan squeals at a pitch that would make dogs cower. Callie and Jack put their arms around each other, look over at Sam and become very emotional.

Marianna smiles as Sam lifts Megan into the new chair, then puts his arm around Marianna as Jack and Callie show her all of the buttons. Megan begins to maneuver around the driveway and does a couple of wheelies. Marianna opens the passenger door, takes out a pink princess helmet and places it on her head. Callie looks at Sam and then gives him a long, heart-felt hug. SSV pats Sam on the back and compliments him.

"You did good, Sam. Really good."

Everyone hugs goodbye and Jack, Callie and Megan drive away.

After another intimate dinner for two in the dining room, Sam drives Marianna home. They seem to never run out of things to talk about and do so with Christmas music setting the tone on the radio and SSV comfortably sitting in the back seat.

Marianna says, "This has been an amazing few days. Becca would love every gesture of kindness that you have arranged!"

Sam replies, "Well, I gotta say that I finally understand why she loved giving so much."

SSV chimes in from the back seat.

"Finally! Hallelujah!"

Sam gives SSV a playful, even semi-welcoming look of "OK enough!" in the rearview mirror.

They arrive at Marianna's house. Sam opens her car door for her and arm in arm, Sam walks Marianna to the door. He stops just short of the steps and playfully dances with her. She laughs and loves every second of it. In conclusion, he twirls her, then bows. She curtseys. He walks her to the door, pulls mistletoe out of his pocket and holds it over her head. They kiss. SSV, still in the backseat of the car watches them and smiles approvingly.

Chapter 14

It's a gorgeous, crisp, winter morning. The sky is the bluest of blues and not a cloud anywhere in sight. Manny trims back some bushes along the driveway and waves as a stretch limo climbs the winding driveway and parks at the front of the house.

The driver opens the limo doors for Robert Waters, dressed as if for the cover of GQ, and his wife, Tess, a fashion plate dripping in Tiffany's jewelry—both early thirties. Together with their ten year old son, Bobby, looking like an ad for REI, and their eight year old daughter, Chloe, who gets her fashion sense from television and social media trends, they exit the limo. Robert carries a wrapped gift.

Belle opens the front door, welcomes them and everyone enters in. There's a scent of cinnamon potpourri in the air and the sound of Christmas melodies pour in through a very sophisticated Bose sound system. She escorts them into the family room where they are seated. Tess examines her manicure. Robert looks around at the decorations that have been absent for a number of years and Bobby and Chloe play games on their devices.

In the kitchen, Francie places two large loaves of French bread on cookie sheets into the oven. She turns to her workstation, chops vegetables and puts them is a large pouter pot simmering on top of the stove. Belle enters and requests an update.

"How's lunch coming?"

"Most uncomplicated Christmas meal I've ever prepared!"

Francie takes a large spoon and stirs the pot, tastes the broth, then adds a pinch of salt.

A gentle fires crackles in the fireplace of the family room and "O Come, O Come, Emanuel," is heard throughout the house. Under the tree there are no presents, only envelops with names on them. Robert places the gift he brought next to the envelopes.

Bobby puts down his device, goes over to the tree, picks up the envelop with his name on it, smiles and waves it at the rest of the family. Robert motions Bobby to put it back. Chloe, oblivious to her surroundings, continues playing games on her device. Tessa sits, gives the room a visual once over, then admires her rings, bracelet and watch. Sam and Marianna, dressed impeccably, enter and greet everyone.

"Hello everyone!"

Robert and his family all stand and offer insincere hugs and greetings. Robert looks at his watch. SSV observes the interaction and addresses Sam.

"Sure you're ready for all this?"

Bobby spares no words for why he's come.

"Hey, Granddad, I saw the envelop with my name on it. Can I open it?"

Chloe adds her two cents.

"Bet it's cash—and a lot of it. I hope it's enough."

Tess makes her attempt at proper parenting tips.

"Children, don't be rude. Your grandfather is always generous. I don't think you have anything to worry about, do they Sam?"

Marianna sees the disappointment on Sam's face as he attempts to move things forward.

"Hungry?"

Sam motions them all to follow him to the dining room. Jack, Callie, Megan, Aunt Ginny and SSV are seated at the table. When the others enter, they all shout.

"Surprise!"

After exchanging niceties and Robert's family seemingly underwhelmed by the intrusion of the extra family members, everyone sits at the table drinking Wassail and waiting for food to be served.

Robert, Tessa, Bobby and Chloe's cell phones are beside them on the table. Chloe and Bobby are obsessively texting and playing video games. Robert and Tessa periodically pick up their devices and check for messages.

The others sit quietly watching them, disappointed at the lack of interaction. Robert realizes he could better utilize the unscheduled time. He reaches into his breast pocket and pulls out two gift cards.

"We were going to drop these by this afternoon, but since you're here, Merry Christmas."

He gives Megan an Amazon card, and Jack and Callie a Visa card, no envelop, unwrapped. Callie responds with sincere gratitude.

"That's very thoughtful of you. Thank you!"

Robert covers his tracks.

"Aunt Ginny, we didn't know we'd be seeing you. Sorry."

Aunt Ginny elects to be gracious.

"Seeing all of you is gift enough!"

Chloe whispers to Bobby.

"Seeing us is a gift? Never heard of that one before."

Callie reaches in her purse and pulls out four gifts, all the same size, wrapped in different colors of tissue paper. Megan watches with great anticipation as Callie proudly passes them out to the four and enthusiastically awaits their response. They all open them. They are hand-knitted ski caps. Sam, Marianna and SSV smile, admiring the hats. SSV can't contain himself.

"Beautiful!"

Marianna can't contain herself and responds enthusiastically.

"Those are lovely, Callie!"

Due to their obvious lack of manners or the appreciation for the time, energy and thoughtfulness that went into creating the gifts, Jack feels the need to explain the effort that went into making the caps.

"Callie spent a lot of time and love knitting those for your ski trip."

They all seem underwhelmed and not at all impressed. Callie, Jack and Megan look disappointed. Sam, Marianna and Aunt Ginny are appalled with the ingratitude and use immense restraint not to leap across the table and demonstrate first hand the magnified face of ugliness that poor etiquette can take on.

Tess, in a forced and monotone attempt, tries to muster a civil comment.

"That was nice of you, Callie."

Robert echoes the gesture.

"Yeah, it was. Nice. Thanks."

Bobby and Chloe go back to playing with their devices as Sam makes an announcement.

"I've decided to start a few new traditions this year."

Everyone looks curious.

"First, I'd like everyone to cut off your cell phones and give them to Belle."

The family looks like they've just been asked to donate a major organ while still alive and without anesthesia. They look at each other and comply as Belle comes in with a silver tray and goes around the table confiscating the devices.

"Thank you, Belle."

The family squirms looking uncomfortable like a pop quiz is about to be given. Sam continues.

"Now, I'd like to go around the table and have everyone tell one thing for which you are grateful."

Bobby and Chloe look at each other and roll their eyes. Robert and Tessa are equally resistant to the idea. Robert tries to change his dad's mind.

"Dad, really?"

Tess chimes in, "Yeah, Sam. C'mon', it's Christmas! You know, great food and gift giving..."

Sam ignores the resistance.

"I'll start. I am grateful to have the entire family here today, including Marianna.

Chloe points to Marianna.

"Marianna isn't part of our family."

Callie quickly corrects her.

"Chloe, sometimes God gives us what is called extended family. It's family that is a gift to us. Marianna has always been like a second mom to me. So yes, she is definitely family."

Chloe shrugs. Marianna smiles. Sam continues the new tradition.

"Bobby, what are you grateful for?"

"I guess my new golf cart."

Surprised that a ten year old has a golf cart, Sam asks for more details.

"You got a golf cart? What did you do to deserve that?"

Bobby proudly explains.

"I didn't get any F's on my report card."

Grieved at how this pattern of overindulgence has permeated all sense of character building and honor, Sam looks at Robert and Tess, but no words will come. Further convinced that privilege and spoiling is way out of hand, Sam moves on to Chloe.

"OK. Chloe?"

Pouting as thought she's lost a vital appendage, Chloe blurts it out.

"I was grateful for my new cell phone until you took it away!"

"You'll get it back. Robert?"

"I'm grateful for another Christmas in Aspen. Best skiing in the country!"

"Oh, you took mine! I'm grateful for Aspen, too. Can I pick the same thing? Probably not. Let me think," says Tess.

Trying to add humor and oblivious to the superficial, shallow responses, Tess tries to contribute.

"I'm grateful for our trust fund that allows us to go to Aspen! And, to renovate our kitchen while we're gone and have the interior of the house painted! It hasn't been redone for at least a year. It's going to be so much better!"

Sam continues.

"Marianna?"

"I'm grateful to be considered part of this lovely family. Thank you, Callie. And, also for this season of the year when we celebrate the greatest gift of all."

Bobby and Chloe talk amongst themselves trying to figure out what is the greatest gift of all. Marianne notices the confusion and addresses them.

"Jesus. Jesus is the greatest gift of all."

Bobby needs a further explanation.

"Why's that?"

Like a runner who's just been passed the baton, Pastor Jack explains.

"Because God sent Jesus to earth to show us how much He loves us, to teach us how to love one another and to make a way for us to be forgiven any time we mess up."

SSV smiles just as Robert sarcastically responds.

"Spoken like a true preacher."

Megan raises her hand.

"I'll go next. I'm grateful for my new wheelchair! I can do wheelies in it and be in races with other kids!"

Callie follows.

"I'm also grateful to be here with our entire family. I think it would make Mom very happy."

Pastor Jacks turn.

"I'm grateful to be the pastor of such a loving, caring church family and to be able to make a difference in our community. And, of course, being married to the best wife in the world and having an amazing daughter like Megan makes it feel like Christmas every day!"

Just short of her exploding from the ingratitude and rudeness of Robert and his family, Aunt Ginny takes the high road and attempts to add a little humor to the bleak atmosphere.

"I'm grateful I woke up this morning. At my age, you never know."

Everyone chuckles. Sam looks saddened by many of the responses as Francie and Belle deliver lunch. A large tureen of soup with a silver ladle and two baskets of French bread are placed at the end of the table. SSV observes.

"Hey, where's the turkey?" inquires Chloe.

Sam calmly answers her and offers a life lesson.

For this year's Christmas lunch we're having soup and bread. Something I learned from Jack and Callie is that soup and bread is more than 90% of the world's population will have to eat today."

Becoming upset and to the point of tears, Chloe blurts out her dismay.

"Are we being punished? If this is all we're getting to eat I hope we're on a dinner flight."

Robert reins her in.

"Chloe, don't be rude."

Bobby, a born debater, tries another angle.

"Well, we're not in the 90%, we're in the top 1%? We deserve more than soup and bread. We can definitely afford it."

"Bobby, enough," says Tess.

Bobby makes a face and makes a circular motion around his temple with his index finger indicating he thinks his grandfather is nuts. Sam directs Jack to say grace.

"Let's pray. Jack would you do the honors?"

The family bows their heads accept for Robert, Tessa, Bobby and Chloe who look at each other as Jack prays. SSV shakes his head.

"Dear Heavenly Father. Thank you for this food we are about to receive. Use it to nourish and strengthen us. And be with all who are not as fortunate. Help us to have a heart to give, serve, help and love. And thank you for Jesus, the greatest gift of all whom we celebrate at Christmas and always. Amen."

Francie and Belle begin serving the soup and bread to a mute and disjointed round of lunch guests.

Chapter 15

The entire family has adjourned to the family room for the gift-giving portion of the visit. Sam grabs the envelops from under the tree. Callie, Jack, Megan, Aunt Ginny and Marianna sit like an audience viewing a sold-out performance. Robert, Tessa, Bobby and Chloe hover like vultures awaiting the kill. Robert jumps up and grabs the wrapped gift they brought for Sam.

"Dad, we want you to open your gift first!"

"OK, sure."

Sam opens Robert's box. It's a large tool set, the same thing they gave him last year and the year before.

"Do you like it?" Robert excitedly asks.

"Yes. Thank you."

Robert continues.

"Hope you didn't already have one. You can exchange it."

"Thank you. I'll put it to good use."

Robert seems pleased with Sam's response. SSV shakes his head at Robert's misinterpretation of Sam's comments and the blatant exposure of the lack of thought that goes into his gift giving. Sam launches into his presentation.

"As I mentioned, I'm starting some new traditions this year. No one in this family needs anything. We are all very blessed. So in your honor, I've anonymously given gifts to people in need."

Chloe is not shy about expressing her disgust with this whole concept.

"You didn't give away my new phone, did you? You said you'd give it back."

"You'll get back your phone, sweetheart."

Marianna, Jack, Callie, Megan and Aunt Ginny sit in silence observing as though watching the lions vs. the gladiator. SSV is confident in the gladiator for a full-on victory. Aunt Ginny works hard to restrain herself from putting an end to this entire fiasco. Bobby's bluntness exposes a reality that cuts to the core.

"If we're not getting presents why'd we even have to come here?"

Robert corrects him.

"Show some respect. We don't just come here for presents."

Chloe, too young to hide her real feelings, shares her truth.

"Yes, we do—presents and food."

"Why else would we come?" asks Bobby.

"We come to see your grandfather," says Tess.

"If that's why we come, why didn't we just FaceTime him?"

Aunt Ginny looks like she's about to explode. SSV offers some wisdom.

"Greed and privilege is like a ravenous, rabid, wild animal out of control, Sam. The love of money is the root of all evil. It's gonna take quite a sword to slay this giant!"

Saddened, Sam shakes his head in disbelief and begins opening the envelopes.

"Chloe, in your honor, I started a scholarship fund for deserving kids who are orphans coming out of foster care or the children of veterans."

"But, that's what you got them. What did you get me?"

"Chloe!" Robert says in admonishment.

Chloe crosses her arms and pouts as Sam opens the next envelop.

"Bobby in your honor, I started a job training program at Callie and Jack's church."

"Great, just what I wanted," Bobby says sarcastically with a look of disgust as Sam opens the next envelop.

"Robert, in your honor, I've donated money to help the families of children being treated at The Children's Cancer Hospital."

Robert stares at Sam and then looks downward. Sam opens the next envelop.

"Tessa, in your honor I bought two cows, an ox, seven goats, twelve chickens and a rooster for a village in Uganda."

"Why would you give animals in my name? I'm SO not an animal person!"

"I've gotten to help many more people than these. And, I will continue to do so every chance I have. That honors God and it honors the memory of your mother. Nothing brought her more joy than giving. She always said that giving makes the giver and the recipient think about God's love. Callie and Jack told me that that's why she started an initiative through their church called, Tag Love. It's an acronym for Think About God's Love."

Bored and ready to bolt, Robert stands. The rest of his family follows suit.

"Well, this has certainly been an interesting day," Robert says sardonically.

Sam makes it emphatically clear that he's not finished explaining all of the changes that are about to occur.

"Have a seat. I have a couple more things I need to tell you."

Slightly shocked by his command, everyone complies. SSV stands holding a sword and begins doing maneuvers with it in playful preparation for the resistance.

"Beginning now, I'm requiring that the four of you volunteer one hundred hours a year to charitable organizations. I am also requiring that you make donations totaling $10,000 a year."

SSV and the rest of the family observe the interaction.

"One hundred hours! There's no way!" says Tess.

Sam helps them do the math.

"It's a couple hours a week."

Robert needs clarification.

"When you say you're requiring it does that mean our trust fund privileges are tied to what you're asking?"

"Precisely. Your mom talked about this for years and I never understood. But, now I do and I'm going to help you embrace this life lesson sooner than I did. The joy of giving is something I'm not going to allow you to miss. And Robert, you have two college degrees. Those degrees cost a lot of money. Their purpose was to equip you with the knowledge and skills to get a good job, one that will support your family. You will begin the interviewing process at the front of the year."

"Get a job? Are you kidding? But, I don't need a job. I have a trust fund!"

"Had, Robert. You had a trust fund. And you still do. I'm just adjusting your access to it. It's important you understand the value of a dollar and what it means to work hard and accomplish goals that you have to work for. I've given you everything with no requirement from you. I was wrong to do that. It has made you lazy and entitled. I'm correcting my mistake. And I apologize for not being a better Dad."

The family stares like deer in headlights. SSV holds his sword in one hand and simulates dropping the mic with the other.

"Boom!"

Don't we have a plane to catch?" asks Bobby.

Bobby, Robert, Tess and Chloe stand as Belle returns with their devices.

“Enjoy your ski trip and I look forward to getting your written reports on your community service involvement and hearing all about your job search. I assure you, this will change your life!”

Robert’s family slowly files past Sam enroute to the door. As they exit the house they exchange some tepid hugs and good-byes before getting into the limo. As the limo pulls away, the rest of the family wave from the porch until they are out of sight and then go back inside to the warm, welcoming, festively decorated family room.

Belle notices the toolbox.

“They gave you another toolbox, Mr. Sam?”

“Yeah, a lot of thought went into that gift. It’s just like the one that they gave me last year and the year before. But, no worries—I’ll donate it to the job-training program at the church.”

Marianna, Francie and Manny enter the room carrying a plethora of beautifully wrapped gifts and place them under the tree. Aunt Ginny looks on, enjoying the visit with the unspoiled members of the clan.

“Now, let’s open the rest of the gifts!” Sam says enthusiastically.

"How come we don't get envelops?" Megan asks.

"Well, Princess Megan, it's because you don't need to be taught about giving to others and what's really important in life. Your parents have done a great job making sure that you understand that."

"Oh."

Jack sets Megan on the floor by the tree. Marianna gathers a stack of gifts and sets them before Megan. Wide-eyed, she assesses all of the packages.

"All of these are for me?"

"They are! Go ahead, open them!"

Sam sets a couple packages in front of Callie and Jack.

En route to the airport, Robert, Tess, Bobby and Chloe—all on their devices—ride in silence. Without looking up, they converse.

"That was so boring," Bobby mutters in a monotone delivery.

"Yeah, no turkey and no gifts," agrees Chloe.

"Well, let's hope it's just a phase that your grandfather is going through," Robert responds.

"We can only hope," says Tess.

The airport is crowded as the limo pulls up to the curb. Robert, Tess, Bobby and Chloe exit as the driver begins unloading enough luggage for a permanent move.

Back at the Waters Estate, Megan sits in the middle of a pile of wrapping paper wearing a jeweled crown, holding a scepter and wearing a long gold robe with soft lining, trimmed in white faux fur over the top of her clothes. Elated, she does the princess wave and blows kisses to Papa and Marianna. Aunt Ginny blows kisses and waves at everyone, too. Megan laughs.

Callie opens a gift certificate for a year's worth of haircuts at the Buckhead salon. She couldn't be happier!

Megan opens her second gift. It's a keyboard and a gift certificate for piano lessons. She squeals with excitement and can't believe her eyes.

Jack opens a box with several new shirts and sweaters. Megan opens the blue coat she wanted. Callie gets several pair of new shoes. Next, Megan opens a box of assorted new books. And, Callie opens a box with a beautiful new winter coat.

Last but not least, Megan opens a box with a small saddle with her initials on it and a tiny bridle as simultaneously, Jack opens a small box with keys. Megan holds up the bridle and Jack holds up the keys. SSV sits at the piano smiling. Sam explains.

"We need to head outside for more clues to both of those gifts."

Knowingly, Sam and Marianna stand, beaming from ear to ear, as they lead Jack and Callie outside. Megan follows in her electric chair.

In the driveway is a brand new fully equipped van for the disabled parked right next to Aunt Ginny's Rolls Royce. Manny sits in the driver's seat, opens the sliding door and demonstrates the lift by lowering it. Unable to control their emotions and gratitude, Jack and Callie begin to cry and hug Sam and Marianna. Megan does a wheelie. Aunt Ginny gets in on the hug-fest, too, before saying goodbye.

"What a lovely day. Thank you for inviting me along. It's my nap time, so I will bid you adieu."

The family helps her into her car and as she pulls away she sounds off her foghorn and enthusiastically waves out the window. Everyone laughs.

They all migrate around back to the stables. Sam places the new saddle and bridle on a Shetland pony. Jack lifts Megan onto the pony and buckles her in. Jack and Sam lean on the fence and chat and Callie joins Marianna as she leads Megan around the ring. SSV listens.

"Marianna, I see the way my dad looks at you. I think you have captured his heart."

Marianna smiles and listens, at first without response.

'The two of you deserve love and happiness. You were mom's best friend. I never remember you not being here. You're already a part of our family, you know."

Marianna continues listening, nods and smiles. Callie puts her arm around Marianna.

"It means a lot to me for you to say that, Callie. I'm not sure where this is all going. It was quite unexpected. But, thank you for your love and support."

Jack and Sam stand at the fences slightly stooped over with their arms on the inside watching the girls, especially Megan.

"Megan sure loves horses. I guess it's in her blood," says Sam.

"Callie says her mom and Marianna started riding when they were just kids."

"True. They were inseparable. And I think Becca had Callie on horseback before she could even walk."

"Callie always says Marianna has been in the family as long as she can remember. She's such a kid magnet. You should see her at church. The kids fight over who gets to sit by her. Why do you think she's never gotten married?"

"She says she's waiting for her man to ride up on a white horse and sweep her off her feet," Sam shares with a big smile on his face.

Marianna notices Sam looking over at her. She smiles and waves. Jack, Sam and SSV wave back. Sam notices SSV enthusiastically waving, smiles and shakes his head.

Chapter 16

It's early morning in Aspen, with a fresh powdery snow on the ground. Robert, Tess, Bobby and Chloe ride the ski lift to the top of a run. They jump off, adjust their gear and take to the slopes on the first full day of their ten-day trip.

Aunt Ginny slept in this morning. The extra events of the week have her a little tired. She sits alone eating a midmorning breakfast. Next to her is the always present place setting and an empty chair. Her television is on but muted as she catches a glimpse of an interview with a soldier she recognizes. She increases the volume.

It's Captain Harry Martinez being interviewed from Afghanistan. Several members of his platoon flank him as he speaks to the reporter. Aunt Ginny talks to the empty chair.

"Look, Colonel. It's Captain Harry, Diann's husband."

Captain Harry engages with the reporter.

"Yes, there are many of us looking forward to getting home for the holidays."

The soldiers surrounding him smile, wave, give thumbs-up gestures and shake their heads affirmatively. S u d d e n l y , bombs and gunfire sound off. The camera shakes and Harry pulls the reporter on the ground out of way. The screen goes black. Aunt Ginny is horrified and prays a simple prayer.

"Oh, Lord please let them all be ok. Please Lord."

National news stateside breaks in and the news desk reporter gives an update.

"An interview with Captain Harry Martinez and some members of his platoon was just interrupted by the sounds of bombing and gunfire. We have lost our transmission signal. But, we will keep you updated as we receive further information."

Next door at the Martinez home, Diann and the children, shaken, scared and gripped by paralyzing fear, stare at the television. The kids begin to cry. Diann can't contain her own emotions but tries to comfort and reassure them.

As the day progresses and the news spreads, friends begin to show up at the Martinez home. Multiple cars are parked out front.

Diann, her children, Janee, Callie, Jack, Megan, Sam, Marianna and Aunt Ginny sit together trying to console the Martinez's as Jack leads everyone in prayer. Diann expresses her frustration.

"I just wish someone would call and give us an update. We just need to know something."

Aunt Ginny's phone rings. She answers.

"Well, finally! Yes. Yes. And how long will that take? Ok, well we're all expecting him home for Christmas. I understand. I expect you to do whatever it takes to make that happen. The buck stops with you. Thank you. And, Merry Christmas to you and the family. Alright. Good bye."

Everyone sits in silence awaiting an explanation. Aunt Ginny explains.

"Amazingly, there were no casualties. But, several of the soldiers suffered from shrapnel injuries, including Harry. He's safe and being treated. Travel plans are on hold until he's stabilized. Not sure yet how long that will take. But, we'll be advised on a need-to-know basis."

Everyone continues to stare at her in silence. After a long pause Diann asks what everyone else is wondering.

"May I ask who that was, Aunt Ginny?"

Aunt Ginny stands and heads toward the door. Exercising manners, Sam, Jesse, Matthew and Jack stand. With her voice trailing off, Aunt Ginny responds.

"It was the President."

Desiring clarification, Diann pursues further information.

"The president of?"

Answering her matter-of-factly Aunt Ginny settles everyone's curiosity.

"The United States. The Commander-in- Chief. I have to go have my nap. I'll let myself out. Diann you're in my prayers. And, if I hear anything more I will let you know."

As she exits, everyone stares at each other trying to get their minds around her last statement.

It's now early afternoon and the day Marianna has set aside to visit Becca's grave. It isn't something she does often, but once a year at Christmas she always pays a visit. It's always an emotional time reflecting on the years of memories and the continued sting of such a great loss.

Solemnly, Marianna places a white poinsettia on Becca's grave and then sits before her marker. Tears stream down her face. Unbeknownst to her, Sam, holding a red poinsettia has come for a visit, too. Respectfully he keeps his distance as he listens to her monologue.

"I miss you, everyday, Bec. But, this time of year it's always worse. Christmas is not the same without you. It never will be."

Marianna begins to sob uncontrollably as Sam draws closer, still listening.

"Some things get easier, but try as I may, I know that I will never find another best friend. There's just no one else like you, Bec. Never has been, never will be. And that keeps me feeling sad. You left a big hole in my heart, Bec, a big empty space in my life, and I don't think that will ever get better. Oh, how I miss you."

Extremely moved, Sam quietly sits down beside her and puts his arm around her. She rests her head on his shoulder, no words, just an understood mutual grief and loss that no one understands better than the two of them.

It's early evening now and Aunt Ginny is on the phone. The TV is on as she sips tea and listens to the person on the other end of the phone. The conversation concludes. She hangs up and dials Diann.

Diann and the kids huddle together on the couch as Diann's phone rings.

"Hello?"

"Diann, it's Aunt Ginny. Harry is stable and will probably be allowed to call you soon. But, it's not likely that he will be able to travel yet. Just be patient and thank God he's ok."

"OK. Thank you, Aunt Ginny."

Chapter 17

After a good night's sleep, Sam awakens early, full of energy and ready to make this day a memorable one. He stands before a large mirror looking like a cowboy, hat and all. SSV looks on approvingly. They do a fist bump.

Desiring an early morning ride, Marianna arrives an hour and a half before she's due for work to be able to fit it in. She walks her horse out of the stables, mounts it and rides through the pasture into the open acreage toward the lake. Once there, her horse slows down to a nice, easy walk. The sun bounces off the water. Marianna dismounts, ties her horse to the fence and drinks in the beauty of the early morning, majestic sunrise.

Suddenly, from a distance, she hears the sound of galloping hoofs. She turns to see Sam riding toward her on a white stallion and dressed like a cowboy. Marianna, completely taken aback, begins smiling and tearing up simultaneously. Sam, smiling broadly, catches up to her and dismounts. SSV sits on the back of the horse as Sam walks toward Marianna, frozen in time, standing by the fence.

Sam stands face to face with her, pulls a ring box out of his jacket pocket and drops to one knee. Marianna gasps and cups her hands to her mouth. Sam opens the ring box to reveal a three carat square diamond. He asks her to marry him. Marianna shakes her head, "Yes." Sam places the ring on her finger, stands up and they have a long, passionate kiss.

Sam's phone rings.

"Hello? Yes. Oh no. Yes, of course. We'll be expecting you. Bye."

"Everything ok?"

"Apparently, Robert attempted a ski jump he's not yet mastered."

Late afternoon a limo pulls up to the Waters Estate. Tess, Chloe and Bobby exit the car. They stand just outside the vehicle and after a few moments, a leg in a cast extends out of the rear door followed by crutches and then Robert. The limo driver begins unloading the luggage as Sam and Marianna come out of the house, offer welcoming hugs and lend a hand. Tessa launches into her editorial.

"We are renovating our house and having it painted. Right now it's full of dust and soon to be full of the scent of fresh paint and we can't stay there for another week. So, well..."

Awkwardly, balancing on his crutches, Robert weighs in.

"We could have gone to a hotel, but since you've cut our budget, well, here we are."

"Glad to have you," says Sam.

Pointing to the kids' duffle bags.

"Kids grab a bag or two. You're old enough to help unload the car."

Bobby eagerly informs his grandfather.

"We're used to our servants doing that for us!"

"Yeah," Chloe concurs.

Looking at her manicure, Tess weighs in.

"I don't want to break a nail."

Sam and Marianna look at each other shaking their heads. Sam gives Robert a look as Robert points to the bags with one of his crutches and almost falls over.

"You're far from helpless. Do as your grandfather has asked."

"And when you're finished, we have a surprise!" Sam explains.

Not wanting to reveal the engagement just yet, Marianna offers a different surprise.

"Yes! You've all arrived back just in time for the church Christmas play!"

Tessa, Bobby and Chloe look less than thrilled as they reluctantly pick up bags and begin making their way inside.

Chapter 18

It's the evening of the annual Midtown Church Christmas Play. The church is packed and festively decorated. Sam, Aunt Ginny, Janee, Rich, Robert, Bobby, Tess and Chloe sit together. Megan wheels up to their pew and addresses Chloe and Bobby.

"Chloe, we have an emergency. We need your help. Mary got the flu and we need someone to take her place."

"I've never been in a play."

"All you have to do is put on Mary's clothes and hold baby Jesus. It will really be easy. I promise."

Chloe agrees and comes out of the pew. Megan addresses Bobby.

"Bobby?"

"Don't even try it. I am not going to be in a cheesy church play."

"Bobby, one of our shepherds is throwing up in the bathroom. He caught stage fright. We really need your help."

Aunt Ginny turns to Bobby and gives him "the look" and a piece of advice.

"Don't make me have to get up!"

Realizing that Aunt Ginny is not someone you want to cross, he complies.

"Fine."

The stage looks like the little town of Bethlehem. The combined children's and adult choir, directed by Diann and accompanied by Callie sing, "O Little Town of Bethlehem."

Chloe as Mary, Joseph and baby Jesus in the manger are center stage, flanked by Matthew, Jesse and Bobby as shepherds, three wisemen and Magi. Harper and Megan in her wheel chair, both dressed as angels, approach a microphone to the side of the stage. Harper begins.

"For unto us a child is born, unto us a Son is given; and the government shall be upon His shoulders,"

Waving her arms and with the forceful cadence of a preacher, it's Megan's turn.

"And His name shall be called Wonderful, Counselor, Mighty God, Everlasting Father, Prince of Peace!"

The combined children's and adult choir, directed by Diann and accompanied by Callie, with Janee singing the solo, perform, "King Jesus is His Name."

"King Jesus Is His Name"

Music and Lyrics by Donna I. Douglas and Babbie Mason

Run and tell everybody you see

Bethlehem has a little baby

Born in a stable late one night

Underneath a sky so starry bright

The star made the night shine like day

And the shepherds came to bring Him praise

Wisemen brought Him beautiful gifts

They brought gold, myrrh and frankincense

What did they call that little, bitty baby

King Jesus is His name

What did the heavenly hosts proclaim

King Jesus is His name

Who would have thought this tiny lad

Would hold all power in his hand

Tell me what did they call Him

King Jesus is His name

The people came from all around

They knelt in awe of this King they'd found

The manger held such a holy sight

This gift from heaven would bring them life

Life forever in a heavenly place

For every nation, color, every creed and race

This little baby's going to change the world

In the hearts of men, women, boys and girls

What did they call that little bitty baby

King Jesus is His name

What did the heavenly hosts proclaim

King Jesus is His name

Who would have thought this tiny lad

Would hold all power in his hand

Tell me what did they call Him

King Jesus is His name

Lorenz/ Pamela Kay Music (ASCAP) adm. by EMI/ MaySun Music (ASCAP)

Pastor Jack takes the stage.

"What a great job everyone did sharing the Christmas story. For thousands of years, prophets had foretold this Savior, the Messiah that God would send to earth. This is why we celebrate!"

" Jesus came to teach us how to love, how to forgive, how to have peace in any situation and how to live life to the full. Our sin has separated us from Holy God. We need forgiveness for all of our transgressions. Jesus gave His life on a cross to pay for the sins of the world."

"He offers us a gift, the gift of forgiveness, salvation and reconciliation to God the Father through placing our trust and faith in His great sacrifice on the cross. That sacrifice was made out of His great love for us and on our behalf."

"We here at Midtown Church hope—if you never have—that you will consider receiving the greatest gift of all: forgiveness of your sins and redemption through Jesus. Jesus said, "For God so loved the world that He gave His only Son, that whoever believes in Him shall never die but will have everlasting life. For God did not send His Son into the world to condemn the world but that the world through Him might be saved."

"As my pastor friend, Andy Stanley, says, "Following Jesus will make your life better and make you better at life." If you are interested in learning more about Jesus and the gift of salvation, please ask me or any of our greeters or fill out the card in the pew, place it in the prayer request box at the back of the auditorium and we will happily contact you. Now, please stand and sing along with our choir this beautiful Christmas song, "Joy to the World."

At the conclusion of the song, Diann takes center stage.

"Please be seated. We hadn't planned to include this last song. But, a few days ago, we got word that a roadside bomb in Afghanistan injured my husband, Captain Harry Martinez. He was supposed to be home for Christmas and in fact, that's all that Jesse, Matthew, Harper and I wanted for Christmas. It doesn't look like that will happen.

But, hopefully he will come home soon and we're grateful that he is ok. There are many serving our country just like Harry. So I'd like to sing this song, which will serve as our closing prayer, in honor of Harry and all those like him. It's titled, Peace on Earth."

Diann sings, "Peace on Earth."

"Peace on Earth"

Music and Lyrics by James Casto and Donna I. Douglas

It's been a really hard year

Many more heartaches than we bargained for

So much loss all around us

Between hurricanes and desert wars

To be perfectly honest

I'm ready for December to end

Pack away all these nightmares

And dream again

Learn to dream again

I don't have a long list of things I don't need

What I want costs more than I deserve

So Jesus if you're listenin' on Christmas Eve

We could use some peace on earth

We could use some peace on earth

So many hearts have been broken

Shattered by life's unexpected turns

Beaten down but still hopin'

The prayers they pray

Are being heard

I don't have a long list of things I don't need

What I want costs more than I deserve

So Jesus if you're listenin' on Christmas Eve

We could use some peace on earth

We could use some peace on earth

O Prince of Peace

It's You we need

Among this chaos

And all this debris

I don't have a long list of things I don't need

What I want costs more than I deserve

But, Jesus if you're listenin' on Christmas Eve

We could use some peace on earth

We could use some peace on earth

At the conclusion of the song, the squeaky double doors at the rear of the auditorium open. Everyone turns around. Captain Harry Martinez, on crutches, enters and slowly makes his way down the aisle. Diann, Jesse, Matthew and Harper run toward their Dad and embrace him. Jack steps to the mic and looks upward.

"Thank you for hearing our prayers, Lord! Everyone, please welcome home, Captain Harry Martinez!"

Everyone bursts into applause. Even Robert and Tess are moved. Marianna and Sam, both applauding, lock eyes and wipe the tears. SSV applauds wildly. Diann looks past Harry to find Aunt Ginny. She spots her and whispers to Harry. They turn and approach Aunt Ginny and give her a long hug. Harry addresses Aunt Ginny.

"Thanks for the ride home. I understand you made all of the arrangements."

Diann looks curious and Harry tells her the secret. The kids listen in.

"My ride home was on Air Force 1."

Beaming, Diann looks at Aunt Ginny and shakes her head in complete amazement. The kids look at each other wide-eyed as Aunt Ginny responds.

"The President wasn't using it, so why not!"

Attempting to bond with her, Jesse offers up a question.

"Aunt Ginny did the Colonel help to arrange the ride?"

"No, precious boy. The Colonel died. He only drops by during meals, to watch Wheel of Fortune or when we need a fourth player for bridge. Other than that, he's permanently in heaven with Jesus. It was the President. The President arranged the ride."

Still not completely convinced, Jesse seeks further clarification.

"The current President of the United States? Or one who's no longer with us?"

"The current President of the United States—a personal and longtime friend. He and the Colonel were roommates."

Concerned about the time lines, Matthew chimes in.

"Roommates recently?"

"In college, boys. They were roommates in college."

Jesse and Matthew enjoy a long sigh of relief.

Chapter 19

It's Christmas day and the Waters Estate is busting with more love, joy and celebration than it's seen in years. Megan, Chloe and Harper, all dressed up as princesses sit at the piano singing, "Joy to the World." Marianna, Callie and Tess shoot video from their phones and cheer wildly as the song concludes.

Marianna takes a turn by sitting down and playing "Fur Elise" as Chloe, Harper and Megan pretend to be ballet dancers. Megan holds up one arm, spins in her wheel chair to match the moves of the others and doesn't miss a beat. Standing against the wall, SSV takes in all of the family bonding and notices unattended cell phones on the coffee table.

Sam, Jack and Robert, who masterfully balances himself on crutches, show Bobby, Matthew and Jesse how to brush a horse and saddle it. The boys lead their horses out of the barn into the corral and Sam helps them mount up. As the horses start to trot the boys smile broadly and then burst into laughter.

Sam, Robert and Jack stand together at the fence watching the boys. Sam wedges himself between Jack and Robert and puts his arms around the shoulders of both. SSV sits on the fence observing with great satisfaction.

Diann and Harry—on crutches—ride a golf cart as they approach the lake. They stop, embrace and have a long, sweet kiss.

Inside in the media room, there are twelve oversized reclining chairs and an 8x10 foot movie screen, playing, "It's a Wonderful Life." Janee and Rich, snuggled together, sit dead center, eating popcorn and drinking hot cocoa.

The sound of a blaring foghorn is heard in the distance. Aunt Ginny, driving slightly faster than she should, speeds down the driveway of the Waters Estate toward the house and parks out front.

It's nearing time for Christmas dinner and Sam has given the employees the day off. However, they prepared the full feast. It just has to be warmed up and served. The entire family and guests help warm up turkey, dressing, gravy, mashed potatoes, green beans, cranberry sauce and rolls. Robert, Tess, Bobby and Chloe wear their homemade ski caps. One by one, each item is placed in serving bowls and on platters.

Every seat is filled at the dining room table. It is a beautiful sight indeed. Robert, Bobby, Tess, Chloe, Callie, Jack, Megan, Janee, Rich, Diann, Harry, Jesse, Matthew, Harper, Aunt Ginny, Sam and Marianna. Although everyone expects Sam to assign the saying of grace to Pastor Jack, or Callie or even Marianna, he doesn't. Instead, as the fully restored patriarch of the Waters family clan, he leads in a grateful prayer of thanks and celebration. SSV proudly observes. Following, everyone begins consuming the beautiful meal, chatting, laughing and enjoying this long overdue time together. Everyone eats, chats and has a great time.

As dinner winds down, Sam and Marianna stand at the head of the table. Sam makes a toast, and clicks glasses with Marianna, who holds up her left hand to show off her ring; then he gives her a kiss. Everyone raises their glasses and then applauds. Callie get up from her chair and makes her way to hug Marianna and her Dad. Megan and Aunt Ginny blow kisses.

Slowly, Sam takes in a panoramic view of each of the faces and activities of every family member and friend seated around his table. SSV smiles and nods proudly as he recognizes Sam and all of the hard work and progress he's made.

"Welcome back, Sam. Merry Christmas!"

Sam winks and hoists his glass in SSV's direction.

"Merry Christmas!"

To download the soundtrack of five original songs from Finding Christmas please visit:

www.donnadhere.com

"Finding Christmas"

Music and Lyrics by Donna I. Douglas and Cheryl Rogers

It's more than a time
For getting together
With family and friends
More than stockings by the fire
Twinkling lights and decorations
More than Santa Claus
Or candles and wreaths
So much more than all the presents
Underneath the tree

Finding Christmas
Changes everything
No more searching
No more wandering
It's comfort and joy
It's hope and peace
And love just waiting to be found
By opening this perfect gift
And finding Christmas

A star in the East

Lit up the heavens

For this newborn king

A manger in a stable

Became a throne where angels sang

Shepherds and wisemen

Bowed down before the Christ

The Savior God had promised

Was right before their eyes

Finding Christmas

Changes everything

No more searching

No more wandering

It's comfort and joy

It's hope and peace

And love just waiting to be found

By opening this perfect gift

And finding Christmas

Dear Friend,

Thank you for reading, Finding Christmas. I hope that you enjoyed it and were reminded by a simple children's church play that Jesus came to earth as a baby in a manger. But, He left the earth as a resurrected King and is alive, well and seated at the right hand of God the Father. in heaven.

My prayer is that you, your family and friends personally experience the peace, joy, love and forgiveness that Jesus came to earth to freely give us. There is no better gift and it's what makes Christmas worth celebrating!

Merry Christmas and may your new year be your best so far!

Big hugs,

D

Made in the USA
Monee, IL
04 November 2019